The
Courtship of a Careful Man
And a Few Other Courtships

"'OH, NOTHING, DEAR, BUT THAT I DARE SAY IT WOULD SUIT ME'"

[See p. 28

The
Courtship of a Careful Man
And a Few Other Courtships

by
EDWARD SANDFORD MARTIN

Short Story Index Reprint Series

BOOKS FOR LIBRARIES PRESS
FREEPORT, NEW YORK

First Published 1905
Reprinted 1970

STANDARD BOOK NUMBER:
8369-3599-3

LIBRARY OF CONGRESS CATALOG CARD NUMBER:
77-125232

PRINTED IN THE UNITED STATES OF AMERICA

Contents

Illustrations

The Courtship of a Careful Man

The Courtship of a Careful Man

HEOPHILUS BRONSON sat before the fire with the evening paper in his lap. Apparently he was comfortable. Actually he had his back to the wall and was fighting it out, and was considerably worn with the stress of conflict. Of all hard things that are part of the common lot, and which persons with the greatest dislike for disturbances cannot hope wholly to escape, the hardest is to choose, at a critical point, between two courses. Work is a simple matter enough once it is blocked out. One has only to measure one's strength and wit against the daily strain, and the special obstacles, and take what comes, be it profit or be it loss. Work conserves and buttresses equanimity, but

3

The Courtship of a Careful Man

to make up one's mind in a crisis, where there is everything to be considered and time to consider everything—oh, that is the very devil! Back and forth the tumult was raging in the mind of Theophilus as he sat in apparent repose. Back and forth it had raged for days together, doubt grappling with hope, and misgiving tripping up determination as often as it found its legs. In the confidence that comes from two cups of coffee at breakfast the way would open so clearly that it seemed the only way, but the late-in-the-afternoon mistrust that follows the day's expenditure of nervous force would settle down like a fog and obscure everything. He had come to the point when he no longer regarded himself as a single positive force which was trying to arrive, but rather as a sort of human gridiron over which a big game was in progress, the issue of which no fellow could predict. He hated being a gridiron. He detested being so torn up and trampled upon. To be a nice green meadow, with a tranquil stream purling down through it, was what he liked, and here he was, ravaged from morn till

4

eve, and even in hours when he ought to be asleep, by this desolating combat, which he could not escape. The most that he knew was that before he was quite dead the thing would come to an end and he would commit himself to something. He knew also that once committed he would stick. It was confidence in that that held him, for in that lay his only assurance that the issue of such violent inward strife would be of importance enough to pay for the quest. What was it all about? He was trying to determine whether to invite Eleanor Cunningham to marry him.

He stirred. He sighed. He got up and filled a pipe. "I shall have to advise with her about it," he muttered to himself, and sighed again, and blew a cloud, and sat down and read the paper.

It is a serious thing to be thirty-five, and old of one's age, and feel constrained to get married. Love at twenty-two comes away from one easily, like children's milk-teeth, but the second teeth come away hard. Theophilus was not at all disposed to fall in love. He had done it in early life, and though falling in love is always a valuable experience—provided it doesn't happen periodically, like fits—his had hurt him and made him wary. He didn't want to fall in love again. He wanted to get married. He knew it was time, and even past time. He was a discreet, observing person, with a habit of reflection, and he realized that if he kept on in the celibate state he would come to no kind of good that would satisfy him. Moreover, after due searching of the spirit, he had about concluded that of all the women he knew Eleanor Cunningham was the one likeliest to make him happy if she would. If she would! It had come to the point where that was the main trouble.

He stopped to see her on his way up-town the next afternoon. She gave him tea and refreshed his spirit with discourse. He liked it amazingly; the more because the fountain of his own thoughts did not incline to overflow.

"Do you know," he said to her, finally, "that I contemplate getting married?"

"So?" she cried. "Great news! And who

is the happy lady? Let me think: Lalage,
Neæra, Cloris, Lucy, Margaret, a girl from
Chicago, a Boston girl, an old love? Who has
been setting snares for my friend Theophilus—
Theophilus the fancy-free?"

"None of them," he answered; "no snares
at all."

"Is it any one I know?"

"I will tell you next week. But don't expect too much. It is only a provisional intention, and it may come to grief."

"Come in next Wednesday and tell me," she
said; and with that he betook himself off. As
he went up the street he stopped at a florist's
and sent her the most ingratiating flowers he
could find. But she sat still and alone, and
meditated; and as she meditated, idly, she
poured out of her cup the few drops of tea that
were left in it, and noticed a shred of tea-leaf
that stuck to the side.

He went to church the following Sunday, and
sat where he could see her. Outside the church
he met her. "Thank you for the flowers," she
said. "I received them as a consolation prize.

7

The Courtship of a Careful Man

But what are you doing here? Where the treasure is, there look on a Sunday morning for the heart and the man. Have I overlooked any one?"

"I guess not," said Theophilus. "I saw only you."

He reappeared on Wednesday.

"Now," said Eleanor, "I am to hear who the lady is?"

"What lady?"

"The girl you are going to marry."

"I'm not sure there is one."

"But you said you were going to marry!"

"No; I only said I contemplated it."

"Even that presupposes a girl!"

"Yes."

"Well, don't keep me in suspense. Who is she?"

"Do you really want to know?"

"Yes; yes!"

"Ever so much?"

"Ever so much!"

"And won't tell a soul?"

"Not a living soul."

8

The Courtship of a Careful Man

"And will take it kindly?"

"Like an angel."

"Well, bear up, then. Since you will know, it was you. I was thinking I'd marry you, if you didn't mind."

"Come! no evasions. Who is it?"

"Just you; nobody else; just you. Do you think well of the idea?"

"Not at all. You knew I wouldn't have you. Pshaw! You really made me think you were engaged."

"No, I'm not. But it is true that I hope to be."

"To whom?"

"To you. As I said before, to you."

"Incorrigible! Haven't you been courting any one at all?"

"Only you."

"I don't believe it. Yes, I do, if you say so. But you haven't courted me."

"How can you say so! Five, six, seven long years have I been unobtrusively faithful. Fourscore and eleven balls and receptions I have been to because you were there. Sevenscore and thirteen gatherings I omitted to attend because you were not going. Only last week I sent you some roses, and this makes twice I have been to see you in five days. If that is not courtship, do tell me what your idea of courtship is, so that I may buckle to and try to realize it."

"So shall I not. You ought to know that who lays his snare according to the plans of the bird catches nothing. So there was no girl, after all. Well, I do not grieve. After all, the marriage of a good—even a fair—bachelor involves a loss to society."

"No doubt a good-sized squad of unattached men—'loose men,' Mrs. Rhinderpost calls them —is a convenience to ladies who give dinners, but do not deceive yourself about the unattached state. It may be laudable at twenty-five, but it is discreditable at thirty-five, ominous at forty-five, and desperate after fifty. A true friend should encourage a friend to get himself saved before it is too late."

"Have I discouraged you?"

"May I speak to your father, then?"

10

The Courtship of a Careful Man

"Surely. But not about me. How impertinent you are!"

"Oh no; only old and out of practice. It is so long since I have courted any one but you. You, to whom each season continues to bring its appointed victims, cannot realize how rusty the persuasive arts grow by disuse."

"Maybe the dissuasive art does, too. I suspect so sometimes when I see the men some women marry. Which of us knows what is in store? Even at twenty-seven one is not sure of one's future."

"Not quite; but some women are terribly wise at twenty-seven, and of course it is a grave matter to court a woman who has grown wise and keeps her wits about her. I suppose that once she has put her illusions into storage she hesitates to get them out and back into her life."

A week later. The same to the same:

"Would it interest you, ma'am, to know that my landlord has had notice that my lease, which runs out on May 1st, will not be renewed?"

2.   11

The Courtship of a Careful Man

"That delightful bachelor apartment? How could you! I have always considered it ideal."

"Oh yes, a comfortable place — ideal at twenty-seven, no doubt, but no longer ideal at thirty-five."

"One or two lumps? I would never remember though you drank my tea once a week for a year."

"Two, please. It takes daily exercise to impress such things on the mind."

"Oh, daily practice might do it, no doubt. But where and how do you propose to live next?"

"Who can tell? Several benevolent young real-estate agents are trying to provide me with a house."

"A house! Are you going to housekeeping?"

"You might have inferred that from what I have told you of my desire to be rescued from the odious condition of bachelorhood."

"But you will still be a bachelor, even though you hire a house."

"Perhaps; but no more than I can help. When I have a house and a maid and a man, at least it cannot be said of me that, knowing better things, I prefer worse."

"'And a maid and a man.' Dear me! I suppose you have the man already, but where will you look for the maid?"

"I shall have to look as other helpless men do."

"Get a man and his wife. That's the best way for a lone man."

"Then I shall not do it. The best way for a lone man is not what I am looking for. Maybe I shall have two maids and not a man at all."

"And you feel competent, then, to manage two women and keep a clean house?"

"Far from it. Heaven knows how I shall fare!"

"Where are you going to find a house?"

"Where would you advise me to look?"

"They say there are very good houses up on the west side."

"Do you like it up there?"

"I? No; it's too far from home and friends for me. I like it here where father lives, or else on the east side somewhere not too far up."

The Courtship of a Careful Man

"The upper west side is too remote for a bachelor. I had not thought of going there. The Park Avenue neighborhood between Forty-second and Thirty-fourth Streets is not bad, if one's aspirations and one's income can be successfully adjusted there."

"I dare say. I have friends that find it satisfactory. But they are married."

"Yes; I never heard that being married necessarily made life less supportable in that region, provided one was married to one's taste. That reminds me. Have you had any better offers since I filed mine?"

"Since you what?"

"Since I proposed to you?"

"You didn't."

"My dear lady, you have no memory. The last time was only a week ago. Have there been likelier ones since?"

"None could be less likely; but there have been none likelier—none at all."

"And you are a whole week older, and, alas! wiser by a whole week's experience."

"Comfort yourself. One does not grow

steadily wiser week by week. Wisdom comes by jumps. You go on being foolish for long periods of time, and then grow suddenly wise overnight."

"I suppose that's true. It takes a jolt. Are your summer plans made yet?"

"Father talks of our going abroad for six weeks."

"That would take you to the middle of July. How about August?"

"Who can tell? Paul Smith's, Bar Harbor, somewhere. We are such a small family that we don't settle to anything beforehand. It may be Newport, if father has to keep near town. Could it possibly be you, sir, that I have to thank for the anonymous flowers that come to this house from day to day?"

"It might. Who can say? Do they please you?"

"They are lovely. They excite the admiration of this household; also its curiosity. But what an extravagance for a man who is about to move into a house!"

"Oh no; I put it all down to necessary expenses in furnishing. When you buy a new

The Courtship of a Careful Man

frock you don't try to save money on the trimmings, do you?"

"Indeed I do; but it is so hard to do it that
I usually get the trimmings first, and try to save
on the rest."

"I wish I could. But you are so obdurate.
At least you realize that I realize that the
trimming is the more important. Thank you
for that."

"Thank me for very, very little. I realize
chiefly that you are persistently saucy."

In the passenger-list of the *Plutonic*, which
sailed from New York to Liverpool. on May
29th, were the names of Mr. and Mrs. Charles
P. Cunningham and Miss Eleanor Cunningham.
In the list of the *Omaha*, which sailed on June
19th, was the name of Theophilus Bronson.
That was how it happened that a lady who
was inspecting the National Gallery in London,
on the morning of June 26th, exclaimed in
tones of surprise, as she held up her hands:
"Theophilus, of all men! When did he come,
and what brought him?"

The Courtship of a Careful Man

"Yesterday, by the *Omaha*, on an errand."

"An errand of business?"

"The most important. To see a lady."

"And have you seen her?"

"Yes; I have found her, thanks to her mother's kindness in telling me where to look. How does she do, and how did she sustain the perils of the voyage?"

"Meaning me, as usual. I do very well, and there were no perils."

"And is she happy here?"

"Perfectly. Delightful weather, delightful shops, delightful sights, and agreeable people. No cloud in the sky, except one that overhangs the New York Custom-house. And you?"

"I am happy, too."

"Do you stay long? Will you come with us to Paris on Saturday?"

"I go to New York on Saturday."

"Three days ashore? Crossed the ocean for a visit of three days?"

"It is all the time I can spare now. I must save something for August and September."

"Why, the trip won't pay you!"

"Who can tell? I thought it would. I planned six weeks ago to come."

"No doubt you needed the voyage."

"I think I could have worried along without the voyage. But, as I said, I had an errand."

"Oh yes: to see that girl. It wasn't worth so much trouble, was it?"

"Amply. I wanted to know what she was doing, and who was helping her. I don't like these spring trips to Europe for girls very much."

"You might have written and inquired."

"Oh, I didn't want to inquire. I wanted to know. It costs five cents to inquire, and you are apt to get back about five cents' worth of information. Besides—"

"Well?"

"Perhaps I am foolish to tell you, but—well, I feared the girl distrusted the completeness of my infatuation."

"Oh!"

"And as I am a conventional person, and have passed the age of violent indiscretion, and

18

The Courtship of a Careful Man

live in New York, and cannot stand within eyeshot of Fifth Avenue and sing to a guitar by moonlight under her window, I had to use such means as the times permit."

"Yes?"

"And, besides, I got restless. It is a serious matter to get restless at thirty-five."

"Of course you were restless. What could you expect after giving up an apartment where you had lived for seven years? Have you got a house yet?"

"Not yet. There seems to be no hurry. I have stored my belongings and hired a couple of rooms for the summer."

"I told you you were rash. Of course you were restless."

"Why, the rooms are comfortable enough, and the town is full of clubs. I'm not so deadly old yet that it's a vital matter to me always to sleep in the same place."

"It seems to me that you are disposed to shift part of the responsibility for your impulses. Now that's quite unlike all I have ever known of you. I begin to think you're a

19

dangerous person, with whom it becomes one to be circumspect in one's dealings."

"I fear not. Any surety company in New York will give a bond at its lowest rate that I am sane, solvent, and safe—oh, distressfully safe! As for shifting any part of the responsibility for my moods, I won't be able to do that until I find some being of enough benevolence to assume what I put off."

"That girl you say you came to see, does she show any sign of harboring benevolent intentions of that sort?"

"Not the least. I wish to Heaven I could think she did!"

"I guess not. If I thought she did, I should feel compunctions about gossiping with you so long in this gallery. It's time we moved on, anyway. It doesn't seem to be a favorable morning for pictures."

"Eleanor," said her mother, "Theophilus Bronson was here inquiring for you. Did he find you?"

"Yes, mother. He's coming to dinner."

The Courtship of a Careful Man

"What's he doing in London?"

"He said he came on business. Partly on business, perhaps, like the rest of us."

"How long does he stay?"

"He goes back Saturday."

"He seems in a hurry. What did he want of you?"

"Oh, just the pleasure of my improving society."

"Was that all? For a man who came to London for three days on a matter of business, he seems extraordinarily appreciative of ladies' society. Why, Eleanor—"

"Yes, mother!"

"Well—nothing, except that you and Bronson seem to have more interests in common lately than you used to find."

"I don't know, mother. It's always pleasant to meet one's friends in London."

It had come to be the 29th of August, especially at Paul Smith's, where the culmination of summer means more than it does at humdrum places where people live all the year around. There the first of September is about the height of the season. Many go, but more come. The little yachts race almost daily on Upper St. Regis, and launches and boats ply incessantly from lake to lake through the connecting slews. At the lower end of Spitfire Lake, Eleanor Cunningham reposed with her back to a tree, Theophilus Bronson sat on a log, and the Adirondack boat, which had brought them to a bit of imperfectly preempted land, rested beside a rude landing which marked the beginning of a little-used carry.

"You seem happy up here," said Bronson.

"Surely. Why not?"

"You are happy, then, unless there is some definite, effectual hinderance. Now that shows a fortunate nature."

"Oh, but there are plenty of tangible reasons for being happy: the air tastes so clean; the lakes are so pretty; the boats are so light; my dear parents are so bland and indulgent; and now, to crown all these blessings, I have the company of my friend Theophilus."

22

The Courtship of a Careful Man

"An edifying list of assets, especially the last item. I wish I might be assured that it was not rightly last as being of least importance."

"Oh, I can change the order if you like. But, anyway, it is in good company, and who knows that I did not put it last for purposes of special emphasis?"

"Dear me, how plausibly you put things! Have you had any fly-fishing up here?"

"None. I believe they use worms in August. Why?"

"There is that in you that I am sure would cast a fly to the satisfaction of a trout; but whether you would care to land the fish you hooked is another question. Have you put many back this season?"

"Now you are a little vague, and, I suspect, a good deal saucy. I have not been fishing. Life here is too polite for fishing. I wear my next-to-best clothes, and return the civilities of the Upper Regis aristocracy, and make afternoon calls by boat, and go out to lunch or to dinner, and climb the mountain, and go on picnics."

The Courtship of a Careful Man

"And are the Upper Regis aristocracy kind to you, and do you like their ways?"

"They are very kind indeed, and very nice, and so are their ways. Their dinners are better than dinners ought to be in the wilderness, and to wear even one's next-to-best clothes in a boat on a rainy night is disturbing, but such drawbacks are trivial."

"To be sure; too good a dinner is a bearable hardship, even when you sleep in a tent. But we digress. Am I here to talk about dinners? Please, will you marry me this fall?"

"My, how sudden and unexpected of you! I guess not. Why should I marry you this fall?"

"It would greatly oblige an old friend. That is one good reason."

"I have never married any one for such a reason as that, and I am not going to begin now. Do see how that sail-boat goes over!"

"Hang the sail-boat! Please pay attention. There are other reasons. You are twenty-seven years old. You have got to marry somebody, sometime—at least, it will probably be better

The Courtship of a Careful Man

for you to, if you can suit yourself; but the
longer you wait the harder it will come. Now
I dare say you could marry a better man and
an abler man and a richer man than I, but you
don't seem to be doing it, and though it is not
for me to be cracking myself up, it is of course
possible that you might go farther and fare
worse."

"Dear, dear! Theophilus. What reasons!
Am I so critically old? Come, get in the boat,
and I'll row you back to the hotel."

"No, no, not yet. Of course the reasons are
absurd. No young thing of twenty-seven is
going to marry any man for stated reasons. I
can't furnish you with reasons. Make any excuse for yourself you like, only marry me! I
know *my* reasons well enough."

"Oh yes. *Your* reasons—I know them. 'I,
Theophilus, being thirty-five years old, and feeling mine infirmities to increase upon me, to
oblige an old friend, the same being my other
and more prudent self, am determined, upon
due consideration, and in spite of all that may
reasonably be urged to the contrary, to marry

25

The Courtship of a Careful Man

the maiden Eleanor, if nothing hinders, lest some worse thing befall.' Those be thy reasons, O Theophilus! Come, help me into the boat."

"Oh no! Well, if you will—careful! No, take the stern seat, please, and leave me the oars. Now we're so far apart one needs a megaphone. Go to with your reasons. I'll none of them. They're not mine. *Conspuez* reasons, anyhow. What have they got to do with it? I have but one, Eleanor. I love you! That's why!"

"Love me! So prudent a man go to such rash lengths at thirty-five!"

"I dote on you; I'm just crazy about you! Just marry me once and see if I am not."

"Why, that *is* news! Why didn't you tell me so last spring?"

"I didn't think your mind was prepared for it. And besides—"

"And besides?"

"What was the use of my telling you unless you were going to have me? To love a woman at twenty-two and blurt it out is a relief to the feelings, and no discredit, for at twenty-two

26

The Courtship of a Careful Man

one is not expected to know better. It is different at thirty-five."

"At five-and-thirty it seems to be more convenient that the lady's assurance should precede the declaration."

"Oh yes; far more convenient."

"But I have given you no assurance."

"None, Eleanor. But I cannot withdraw the declaration. It is true—lamentably true, perhaps—that I love you. It seems to have been growing on me. But that was natural. That would have happened to any man who did not grub the tendency out at the first appearance of symptoms. You see, Eleanor, you are a charming woman!"

"Ah, Theophilus! You, too, are a flatterer!"

"Well, as to that, ask your mother. What I have learned about you I have learned apparently to my sorrow."

"You're steering wild, Theophilus. Our slew is to the right. That's better."

"The lady is in haste to be quit of her admirer's company. Have courage. It is not far."

The Courtship of a Careful Man

A long pause. They approach the opening of the slew. "Did you find a house?"

"I had one in mind. I was going to consult you about it."

"Where was it?"

"Oh, hang the house! It was off Park Avenue below Forty-second Street."

"Did you like it?"

"It is not bad. I dare say I shall take it, anyway."

"Is it high stoop or English basement?"

"American basement. Not a bad house for the money."

"Take it if it suits you. Those American basement houses run overmuch to stairs, but still, if it suits you, I dare say—"

"Dare say what?"

"Oh, nothing, dear, but that I dare say it would suit me."

"You! Eleanor—"

"Oh, look out! You're running into the bank. To the right! To the right! Now do be careful!"

"Suit *you*, Eleanor?"

The Courtship of a Careful Man

"Sit still, Theophilus. Don't try to move in this boat. You'll upset us, surely. Sit quietly and row home like a good man thirty-five years old. Poor dear! Why, I always meant to take you when you really asked me. Is it a new house?"

"I have a good mind to tip you over."

"Better not. Caught is not caged. Is it a brick house or stone? To the left; there are two boats coming. There! Of course there is a butler's pantry?"

"Drat the house! It is a modern house, and there is everything in it that belongs in a house of its size. Since it seems to suit you, I'll telegraph to the agent as soon as we get ashore."

"To the right a little. Now you're headed for the landing. Aren't you going to speak to father first?"

"I have spoken to him. I asked if you were a good daughter."

"Well?"

"And he said: 'Too good to lose. I hope you won't get her!' You see he is unsympathetic, so I shall telegraph without waiting. I say, Eleanor!"

"Well, Theophilus."

"If you had made up your mind to take me, what did you make me get back into this infernal boat for?"

"For your sins, dear, and because I wanted to know more about the house before I was committed to live in it."

A Party at Madeira's

A Party at Madeira's

I

 WANT a new dress," said my wife.

"You always do, dear."

"But I need one badly."

"You always do, dear, and deserve one also."

"But I am going to have it, and I know how. I have been to see your friend, Mrs. Hazard."

"Oh! And you have seen her Tennessee Coal and Iron tea-gown, have you? Isn't it splendid! What are you going to buy?"

"It is lovely, and I am not going to buy anything, because I have bought, and I sha'n't tell you what until I see how it comes out. Mrs. Hazard advised me."

"I suppose you have bet your aunt Joanna's

legacy on one of Mrs. Hazard's gambles. It was kind of you, dear, not to ask my advice. Is it to be an evening-gown?"

"It is: a memorable ball-gown."

"And whose ball do you hope to wear it at, dear? It is seven years since we came to New York, and our presence at a ball has not as yet been solicited. Be moderate, sweet—call it a dinner-dress, and be content to eat in it."

"So shall I not. It is to be a ball-gown, and I shall wear it at a ball which shall be my own ball, which you and I shall give at Madeira's tavern for a coming-out party for your daughter Henrietta."

"Mrs. Hazard's tip seems to have given you a vast deal of confidence. The price of a ball at Madeira's must be about a year's rent. When the pool is troubled, do you expect to put me in also?"

"Oh no. We decided long ago that it doesn't do for you to speculate, because a man can't work at his trade and follow stocks simultaneously. You shall have no concern at all. You are merely to lend me the sixteen Ossawatomie

A Party at Madeira's

and Elba bonds that you keep down-town, and
I am going to do the rest. At least, Mrs. Hazard
and I are. Mrs. Hazard is coming to the ball."

"In the T. C. and I. tea-gown?"

"No, indeed. In a Standard Oil ball-gown,
with lots of real lace on it."

"And suppose the market slumps?"

"It might cause delay; but it won't slump.
Have faith, dear heart, have faith."

For some months after that our experience
of life was tinctured with an aleatory flavor.
The Ossawatomie and Elba bonds ceased to be
securities in that they were withdrawn from
the security of the safe-deposit box where they
were idly living down their coupons, and were
handed over to my wife, who duly tied them
on to the tail strings of various kites. I should
not have ventured to risk them myself, for if
they had dwindled or disappeared through my
rash impatience of penury, I should have had to
face my wife, and to live on in the conscious-
ness that she was aware that I had prejudiced
her prospects of future comfort. I am willing to
take chances on my own account, but not for

35

The Courtship of a Careful Man

her. When she chooses to take the risks, it is a different matter, for I am confident my philosophy would be equal to retrenchments which she would apologize for as well as share, whereas retrenchment which I would have to apologize for as well as share might overstrain my fortitude. Oatmeal with a cheerful and extenuating spirit makes a fair breakfast, whereas oatmeal and remorse taste of sawdust. Besides, I didn't believe that in the long-run my wife would lose. She is a cautious woman, and I was sure she would follow Mrs. Hazard's leadership, and I know Mrs. Hazard, and have, on the whole, a good opinion of her capacity as a speculator. She has had experience both in getting in and getting out. It always seemed to me that she was able somehow to command pretty sound advice, and, though she has the experimental temperament, she is decidedly averse to lying awake nights, and I was sure she would not try to make her everlasting fortune between two days at the risk of parting with her stake. I don't know whether or not it is sinful to buy controlling interests in shares that

36

A Party at Madeira's

seem likely to rise, and, though I am sure it is
perilous, the risk for persons who are duly
cautious seems more a risk of losing one's head
or one's patience than of losing a very large
proportion of one's money.

To this day I don't know what those ladies
bought. Some days my wife's spirits seemed
unaccountably high; some days her cheerful-
ness seemed forced. Early in December plans
began to be drawn for ball-dresses for her and
Henrietta. They were duly executed, and before the holidays were over two very ravishing
gowns came home. Cards of invitation came
home one day in a big box, with their envelopes,
and I expected orders to hire one of Madeira's
rooms, but it turned out that the dateline in
the invitations had not been filled in.

"Will the party come before Lent, Araminta?" I inquired.

She was reading the mathematical end of
the evening paper, with lines up and down her
forehead, and an appearance of distrust in
future events well suited to a reader of that
grave journal.

The Courtship of a Careful Man

"I can't say positively yet. It looks to-night a little as though it wouldn't. The Boers are so obstinate, and things keep happening so inopportunely that it's rather a difficult time to give balls just now."

"Those gowns," said I, "would they keep at a pinch over the summer?"

"Oh yes, dear; we can keep the moths out of them, I guess. Though keeping their style in them is another matter."

My wife went around to Mrs. Hazard's the following morning—so I gathered from the flotsam of her subsequent discourse—and I have no doubt they talked over the telephone with persons down-town. Mrs. Hazard has a telephone. I have accused her of having a ticker in her cellar, but she says not. She has a cellar, though, and that is something. Only one family in fourteen has a cellar in New York. My family has always been of the thirteen that are cellarless. That night Araminta and I went out to dinner, and she wore her new dress.

"What!" said I, "are you going to eat in it, after all?"

"HENRIETTA WORE HER NEW FROCK THE FIRST CHANCE
SHE GOT"

A Party at Madeira's

"Oh yes! Balls are very hard on dresses. It is a shame to wear a new gown to a dancing-party, even at my age."

Henrietta wore her new frock the first chance she got, and a lovely sight she was in it. I had a suspicion that the fabrics of both garments were General Electric, and the trimmings American Bridge, but I never got positive information about it.

"You *tell* everything," my wife said.

I never knew a prayerfuler Lent than we had, but no ball followed it. My wife was not depressed, but her mouth developed new lines of decision. I used to ask from time to time if she had blisters yet from holding on. Spring came, summer followed. We all read the papers faithfully and watched the second sound-money campaign. The last month of it Araminta personally supervised—she was back in town again by that time. She hung a sound-money flag out of the window of our flat, and compelled me to march in the sound-money parade, though it was a rainy day. One day, about a month after that, she brought me back the sixteen

39

The Courtship of a Careful Man

Ossawatomie and Elba bonds, and asked me to negotiate with Madeira for the 24th of January.

"For his big ballroom?" I asked.

"How big is it?"

"I don't remember. You may recall that we both went to the opening—they gave away ice-cream; I remember your enthusiasm—but I have never since got above the first floor. How many people do you expect? That will settle the size of the room."

"I should think about two hundred."

"Where on earth are you going to scrape together two hundred people for a dancing-party? It isn't possible that you know fifty dancing people in New York."

"This ball, William, is not so much for dancing people as for people who haven't danced since—oh, since the panic of '93, and who will be interested in dancing just once more before it is forever too late. We don't want to be crowded. Tell Madeira three hundred. You seem not to suspect that Henrietta has some acquaintances."

A Party at Madeira's

"Good Heavens! dear, you *are* in for it. It will be like a handful of pease in a gourd."

Nevertheless, I went next morning and engaged the biggest room Madeira had, and told him my wife would be along down to see about it. The man in charge looked at me dubiously, and he so evidently wanted to ask me for a reference that I asked him if I couldn't pay the hire in advance. That reassured him a little, so that he reluctantly conceded that that would not be necessary. Then I went somewhat gloomily down street and ordered a new double-breasted white waistcoat. Three hundred people! Where would they find three hundred people to dance to our fiddles and drink our champagne? I don't want to pretend that either my wife or I began life in a foundling-asylum, or have lived on the earth forty-nine and fifty-four years respectively without establishing some social relations. We can get four, or six, or even eight people to dine with us, provided we begin soon enough, and they will all be presentable and remunerative people, who eat and drink with consideration, and show

41

The Courtship of a Careful Man

practice in spoken discourse. But three hundred! I put it all resolutely out of mind, determined to be helpful if I could, and to lay up such store of solace as I might against impending catastrophe. And so I plodded on about my business.

The invitations went out in December. I never saw the list, though I contributed dutifully to it out of such capacity as I had whenever my co-operation was invited. It was composed by Mrs. Hazard, my wife, Henrietta, our cousin Augusta, and my son Alonzo, who was at that time pursuing professional studies in the East, and who sent his mother a list of names. My niece, Sarah Joyce, came to town after Thanksgiving, and for a fortnight occupied Alonzo's vacant state-room in our flat. Her enthusiasm for the ball was so magnificent that I began to take heart, though by that time it was determined that, so far as I was concerned, the ball should be a surprise, for my wife at that time was calling me Thomas for my doubts. I saw two full sheets of postage-stamps on her table one day, and if those women didn't send

out at least four hundred invitations their labor
was disproportionate to its results. At any
rate, they got a peck or two of answers every
day for nearly a week. Now and then they
would let me see one, but only acceptances, and
those only from cronies of my own.

It got to be the 20th of January. My wife
said at breakfast that the ball would hold a
few more persons, and if I happened on any
one that I wanted to ask she would be glad
to send him an invitation.

"Is it an appeal to the highways and hedges?"
said I.

"Not quite that, but to the avenues and the
hotels, and possibly the clubs. You are con-
stantly running across people from out of town
whom you want to bring home to dinner. Maybe you will meet some one whom it will be
pleasant to have at our ball."

"The Binghams of Cleveland are due in town
about now. I will stop in at the Hotel Flanders
and see if they happen to be there."

"That particular labor you may spare yourself, for the Binghams have been asked long

4

The Courtship of a Careful Man

ago, and have accepted. But stop in at the Flanders, by all means. You may find some one else."

Herman Joy and his wife, of Boston, were breakfasting at the Flanders when I stopped there. Maybe they will like to come, thought I, so I put off my overcoat and hat and went into the dining-room to accost them, expecting to work up diplomatically to the ball, and let its existence transpire casually.

"Hello, William!" cried Herman. "Is your wife's party making good progress?"

"Gracious!" said I, shaking hands with Mrs. Joy; "how did you know of it?"

"Why, we're coming. Didn't you know it? I have an errand in Washington, and we are going to stop over on our way back."

"Any one else coming from your part of the world?"

"I think so. I don't understand that there will be any general migration, but my recollection is that the Winters said they were coming, and Sam Park, and one or two others.

44

A Party at Madeira's

Any excuse to get to New York is good. You don't seem to be well posted."

I owned that I wasn't, but professed a thirst for information. "My!" thought I; "what a forehanded woman!" I wasn't caught in any more ignorance that day, for when any one I met said "party" to me I gave him his head, and let him believe I knew all about it. On that day and the three following days I met about twenty more or less intimate acquaintances from Cincinnati, Omaha, Chicago, St. Louis, Buffalo, and other outlying districts. About half a dozen of them said they hoped to see me Thursday night, and the rest I invited, and most of them accepted. Mrs. Aspen, of Cincinnati, said she had always wanted to know what parties were like in New York, and I said so had I, and this was our chance, which seemed to be a different answer from what she had expected, so that her face took on the look of one who bites a gold piece to see if it is good. Then I asked if she had her diamonds with her, and she said yes, and her best gown, too, for she had been to the opera; did I think that

The Courtship of a Careful Man

Ohio people saved their best for Ohio? I said it was so much the fashion in Washington to save the best for Ohio that it would have been no wonder if she had followed it in New York.

At the Fifth Avenue, on Wednesday, I discovered Mrs. Wilson of Worcester, and her daughter, and my wife went down to see them that afternoon. "They are coming," she said. "I told them the Broadheads would be there, and that they would find plenty of acquaintances, and Emily Wilson said that if I did not insist that her mother should make up her mind until after dinner on Thursday she would engage to fetch her."

II

In its superficial aspects that ball was doubtless a good deal like other balls, but I own that to me it was altogether extraordinary and of a surpassing interest. I had not at any time been able to take it seriously. It had seemed to me a delightful piece of impudence to give a dancing-party in New York without a license

"WE ALL WENT IN TOGETHER"

from the mayor or the co-operation of Mrs. Van
Pelt or any of the great social powers that we
read about in the newspapers. As a joke it had
amused me in prospect; but jokes that look
amusing sometimes fall flat in execution, and
irresponsible as I was I had tremors of apprehension as to how this joke would be taken. I
asked Rufus Hartley, kindest of men, and of
mature years like me, to come early and hold
up my spirits over the crisis. He has intimate
friends who are of the world of fashion, and has
been to a few dancing-parties every winter for
the last forty years, and even gives them himself sometimes. I felt that I could lean upon
him, and I did. He was in admirable spirits,
and full of confidence, and so prompt in ren-
dering his good offices that his hat-check was
No. 1 and mine No. 2. My wife and I, Henrietta and my niece, Sarah Joyce, drove down
together. Mrs. Hazard's carriage came up as
ours left Madeira's door, and Cousin Augusta's
cab followed hers so close that we all went in
together, a devoted squad fit to make even a
forlorn hope realize its best intentions. Alonzo

was at our heels, and a couple of Sarah's devoted young men were close after him. After
that I ceased to take special notice of rein-
forcements. People came; the band began.
A lot of girls that seemed to know Henrietta
were dancing presently with young men whom
Alonzo seemed to know. My wife was shaking
hands with a procession of people, I was saying "How do you do?" to every one I had ever
heard of, and many others, and Cousin Augusta
and Mrs. Hazard and Rufus Hartley were dif-
fusing themselves about like ice-breakers, leaving motion behind wherever things showed the
least tendency to congeal. By half-past ten
there ceased to be any question that it was a
real party, and I found myself carried along by
a strong current of activity. Indeed, it was so
strong, and so successfully stimulated by Mrs.
Hazard and her husband, Cousin Augusta,
Sarah, and Hartley, to say nothing of my wife,
that I found leisure to draw out and inspect the
assembly. Francis Joy stopped to speak to
me.

"Very interesting party, Bill," he said.

A Party at Madeira's

"Enough people that I know, but lots I don't. Who's that handsome woman yonder in the violet garb and the big sunburst?"

"That's Mrs. Bingham of Cleveland."

"Who's she talking to? I ought to know the man, but I can't place him."

"Charles Waters, the architect. You must remember. He came here from Boston. He built something for the Binghams—a house, or a church, or something. He married here. There's his wife yonder, dancing with Sam Park. She was Miss Ringgold. Her father came here from Baltimore—oh, twenty years ago—and brought her with him. Sam Park has cousins in Baltimore."

"Thanks. I'll speak to Waters."

Hartley came up. "William, who's that benevolent old lady sitting yonder? Your wife introduced me to her. She's got a daughter here somewhere, whom I've met before."

"Mrs. Wilson — Mrs. Wilson of Worcester. She has a son in Chicago, and goes there. He's counsel for the St. Paul, Chattahoochee, and Gulf, and when you were receiver for the—"

The Courtship of a Careful Man

"I remember. I met the girl at her brother's home. Nice girl. I'll go and find her."

Mrs. Hazard was passing. I accosted h r.

"I beg to congratulate you, Mrs. Hazard, on the success of your party, ma'am."

"My party, indeed! But it is a nice party, isn't it? But do tell me who is that tall, clean-shaven man over there? Your wife presented him to me. Mr. Ryan or something; I met his wife, too."

"Tryon. Sempronius Tryon. He came here from Denver. His wife is from Philadelphia, and a great friend of our cousin Augusta. There she is yonder, talking to Jack Penderson. You know he came here from Philadelphia, too."

"And how did the Philadelphia lady meet the man from Denver?"

"At Colorado Springs, of course. She visited a pulmonary relative there. Take note of Tryon, Mrs. Hazard. He is most remunerative in various particulars, and few know more than he about mines."

"So? Thanks. I'll not forget him."

Seeing that Julia Morison seemed to be un-

A Party at Madeira's

occupied for the moment, I went over to her. She is one of Henrietta's contemporaries that I happened to have known since she wore short dresses.

"Would Julia dance a dance with an old man?" said I, and Julia would, and did, and I sat down beside her afterwards.

"I hope," said I, "that your worthy parents are having fun here, Julia."

"I think they are, Mr. Hardy. Father said it was the second dancing-party he had been to since he left St. Paul, and probably the last he would ever adorn, and he has seemed very much disposed to make the most of it. He's over there gossiping with Mrs. Aspen. You know she's mother's half-cousin, and I dare say she's telling him about mother's relatives in Columbus."

Just then Araminta came up and took me away to speak to Mrs. Thompson, who was Miss Jordan of Charleston, until she married one of the Connecticut Thompsons. Araminta has a very soft spot for the Jordans, and I knew it was essential to her comfort that Mrs. Thomp-

The Courtship of a Careful Man

son should be happy at our party, and I did my best, though there wasn't much to do, for she had fallen in with the Bookstavers, who came here, you remember, from Washington after Cleveland's first term. The Thompsons were in Washington for a couple of years along about that time.

Alonzo happened in reach just at that moment, and his mother caught him and exhibited him with maternal pride to Mrs. Thompson. I don't know why she is proud of Alonzo at this stage of his career, when he represents chiefly the nourishment and education that his parents have provided for him, and the clothes that are furnished by a tailor whose bills come to me. But his mother is proud of him, and I admit that he seems to have assimilated the nourishment and the education pretty successfully, and that the clothes fit him, and that he becomes them. I don't know that much more can be expected of him at his age, and indeed I am a little self-complacent about him myself.

"Alonzo," said I, "who's that young chap dancing with Henrietta?"

A Party at Madeira's

"Job Cartright, father."

"Where did you find him?"

"Why, you know Job! Don't you remember seeing him at Class Day? He was in my class. He's from Providence, and is studying medicine here."

I did remember Job, with Alonzo's help.

I took Mrs. Wilson out to supper. "It was very good of you to come," I said to her.

"I am very much astonished to be here, but Emily said I must come, and just brought me. The last dancing-party I went to in New York was at Uncle James's house down on Washington Square."

"They have them there still. I dare say you would find old acquaintances down there."

"Most of my old friends have moved to Greenwood, and I don't know where the rest are, except one at Sing Sing. Other places hereabouts are so changeable. Tell me, who is that gentleman with Emily?"

"Mr. Hartley, a lawyer. Don't you remember a family of Hartleys that used to live in Stuyvesant Square thirty years ago?"

The Courtship of a Careful Man

"Why, bless you! is that Richard Hartley's son? I remember perfectly hearing of Richard Hartley when I was a young girl. He came here from Albany to practise law, and married some one from somewhere in the western part of New York State."

"That's it! Rufus's mother was one of the Garnets, of Canandaigua. His father managed to send down roots in the crevices in Manhattan's rock, and Rufus has lived and labored and prospered here pretty much all his life, and is now one of the oldest residents."

"I haven't seen his wife."

"He hasn't any, and never had, and I suppose that accounts for his being still a resident of New York and being here to-night. When one generation of a family has labored successfully in New York, the next generation is apt to live in a private car. But, you know, matured bachelors are the creatures of habit, and don't readily migrate."

"But plenty of the older New York families still live here."

"Plenty of them have houses here—splendid

ones, some of them—which most of them use chiefly as convenient points of departure. The people who really live in New York are chiefly people like me who work there, and can't afford to leave."

"But you think people don't feel at home here any more?"

"Everybody feels at home here; that's the beauty of the place."

"What's everybody's home is nobody's!"

"I don't know. Mrs. Gray, whom I met the other day, was born here, and lived abroad fifteen years after she was married, and then came back. She hasn't got back to the soil quite, for she lives in the sixth story of an apartment-house, but New York is really home to her."

"Has she got any one buried here?"

"I dare say. Her father, probably, and very likely others."

"That's a test; not conclusive, but a test. We may live anywhere; we may die anywhere. Like as not I shall die in Chicago, on a visit to my son—and, oh! I don't want to be registered

from there—but where we bury our folks, that
is where we are apt to belong."

"Yes; but the trouble is, we scatter our
burials. With grandparents here and there, and
your own parents elsewhere, and your wife's
relatives somewhere else, all the cemeteries get
to seem hospitable after a while, and ties weaken
out of their multiplicity. It doesn't quite ac-
cord any longer with American enterprise to
have two generations of the same family buried
in the same place. It implies a lack of initia-
tive."

"It's the whole country, then, that's restless,
and not New York alone."

"No doubt. New York changes only because the country keeps boiling over into it all
the time. The fire fails not, and into the pot
goes a steady stream from Europe on one side
and all America on the other, and the scum—
oh, the scum keeps rising undoubtedly. When
the juice is pretty well boiled out of the folks
they rise to the top and move on, or their children do, and lucky they are if they have means
of transportation."

A Party at Madeira's

"But the people who own the town? Doesn't any one feel any longer that New York belongs to him?"

"Croker does, no doubt, So possibly does William Astor; but you know they both live in England now. What they like about England is, doubtless, that they don't own it, and are not responsible for the way it is run. And that is very much what we who happen to be living in New York like about New York. New York grows on you, too—if you manage to carry weight enough to avoid being scummed off. Mrs. Ransom—who was the daughter of Darius Cobb of Detroit—who has lived here twenty years, told my wife the other day that after you had lived here ten years or so, all of a sudden it began to be home. It's a pretty shuddery thought, though, to have no home but New York!"

"When it was my home I liked it," said Mrs. Wilson, "and I like it still, and I shall come back as long as my hotel lasts, at any rate. But I'm going to be buried in Worcester. I'd rather be buried in some permanent place."

The Courtship of a Careful Man

Then we both drank a little champagne and meditated, and I dare say we both realized the same truth—that it was time we were abed.

The working-classes began to go home after supper; the young and the faithful held on a while longer; but a little after one Rufus Hartley declared that as there was no ordinance against it, and inasmuch as we had hired the hall, and could control the music, we should dance a Virginia reel. We did it. Mrs. Hazard danced it with me, and Hartley with Araminta. As many of Henrietta's girls as had not been dragged off by inexorable parents had their choice of all Alonzo's young men. Cousin Augusta paired away with Tom Hazard; Sarah Joyce had two partners—she was just getting into the spirit of it, she said—and we had hands across and down the middle with a final blaze of cheerful animation.

"Araminta," said I, as we waited for the night elevator-man to wake up and let us in, "it was a nice party. It did you credit. Did I tell you what I heard Mrs. Aspen say to Mrs. Bingham? She said, 'I have had a good time,

and I have met people from Keokuk and Kala-
mazoo, and every town in the country except
New York.' 'Maybe that's why you've liked
it!' said Mrs. Bingham."

"Pshaw! there were a hundred and fifty people there from New York."

"Yes, but a hundred and forty-five of them
grew up somewhere else. I think that was the
common tie that made the company hang together. It's a great feat to gather two hundred
polite people in a big city who have so much in
common. Think how absurdly impossible it
would have been to do it anywhere else!"

5

The Making of a Match

The Making of a Match

RS. HERRON sat at a small table in a hotel restaurant. Opposite her was Judge Finch, who had happened in.

"And Susan," the judge was saying, "finds no one good enough for her?"

"Her cousin Matilda describes Susan's attitude as 'choosing.' Very 'choosing,' Susan is nowadays, Matilda says—meaning apparently that she cannot seem to make a choice. We used to call it 'difficult.'"

"New girls, new language, but apparently the same situations."

"I don't know that Susan is a marrying girl. At any rate, she doesn't seem in the least uneasy in the single state."

The Courtship of a Careful Man

"Oh, well, at twenty-four there's still hope. Susan must be about twenty-four now."

"Twenty-six her last birthday, and the spring and the summer have come and gone since then."

"Gracious! how years pile up! Twenty-six! and the spring has come and the summer is ended, and Susan is not yet saved from herself! Yet she must have had opportunities!"

"Oh yes, opportunities a-plenty: opportunities in town; opportunities in the country; steamer opportunities; opportunities abroad, and on the coast of Maine, and in Washington; late spring opportunities in Florida; private-car opportunities; opportunities in civil life; in business life; possible opportunities in the army and the navy, in the simple life and the life of leisure."

"Dear me! has the poor child been so pestered with followers? She must have formed the fatal habit of rejection."

"I don't mean that she has had such a myriad of offers. An opportunity does not necessarily imply an offer of marriage. Susan hates offers.

The Making of a Match

She says they take away her appetite and make her head ache."

"She stands her possible suitors off betimes, then. I suppose that is possible."

"Usually it can be managed without much difficulty—at least it used to be so—though sometimes it involves a change of base. There are mothers who have to pack their girls up and run away from detrimentals. I rather envy them. When I pack up and run it is because Susan demands a change of environment to save herself the trouble of discouraging some threatening aspirant, usually a fairly eligible one. I have stopped humoring her in that way. I tell her she must just make herself more disagreeable, for I am too old to go straggling about with a runaway daughter."

"Is she learning to put out her thorns?"

"I don't know. It seems to come hard for her to be unattractive. You see, the girl is clever and handsome and amiable, and these are not repellent attributes, however they are managed. I am just tired of her. I wish she would marry and done with it, and so does her father;

The Courtship of a Careful Man

though he dotes on her, and is less concerned about her offishness than I am, because he doesn't want to part with her. Neither do I, but she might better marry if she can suit herself, and for her own sake I wish she would."

"My heart bleeds for you in this trouble. If you think my Arthur might possibly suit her, it might be arranged. But would it suit you?"

"Why not? I'm reasonable enough. The trouble's with Susan. Arthur? What is the child like? Has he made you much trouble? How old is he?"

"He has made me trouble enough, but it has been chiefly the trouble of maintaining him and getting him taught his trade. He's twenty-eight: a suitable - enough age, and he's like— I don't know. He is a good, honest lad."

"Where has he kept himself? It seems a long time since I saw him last."

"He has been learning to be a doctor. He wound up at Vienna, where he stayed a year, and only got back and put his name out this summer."

"Poor you! How very long it takes now!

The Making of a Match

Your back must ache with carrying him. I don't think Susan will ever marry a doctor. She will probably think that if she is going to have a man at all, she must have a whole man to herself, and doctors never can call their souls, or their time, or anything their own.

"I see; one trouble with Susan is that you have over-indulged her. If you have brought her up to think she can have what she wants, no wonder you are in trouble. Do get over that idea. It's very generous in me to suggest Arthur at all. Of course it is no more than a suggestion. If you accepted, I could not contract to deliver the goods, any more than you could contract to receive them."

"I will be more humble. Will it be necessary to detach Arthur from any other object before we bring him in range of Susan, or does he happen to be fancy free?"

"I think he is already detached. So far as I know, all the girls for whom he had a special kindness have married stock-brokers or favored sons while he has been studying medicine. I am really a little uneasy about him. He seems to regard girls merely as possible subjects of profitable diseases, which is horrible."

"Has he always been so?"

"Dear, no! He was almost dangerously susceptible in early life, but being a poor young man he had to get over so many infatuations that I suppose it made him cautious. Perhaps he took something for it. Maybe the disease just ran its course and left him immune—apparently immune—for a time. But now that he is by way of beginning to make a living, a few fresh pangs might soften him up and do him good."

"You quite interest me in Arthur. Perhaps he would make us a week-end visit in the country next week. Does he ride?"

"Oh yes—when he gets a chance."

"Susan rides indefatigably at this time of the year, and I dare say will show your young doctor the country. He will get away from the town for forty-eight hours, anyway. I will write him a note, and trust to you to remind him that he once knew us."

With that Mrs. Herron put down her napkin,

The Making of a Match

gathered up her belongings, and proceeded from the restaurant to do what was left of the errands that had brought her to town.

"I hope Arthur will come," she said, as she took her seat in a cab. "I shall want to see him, whether Susan does or not."

New York is at best only a second-rate place to be in in October. Not that it is so bad. It is no longer hot. It catches some brilliant days, when the air tastes fairly good in spite of all the dust and all the flavors of the city. But the better the day and the better the air, the more do rightly constituted persons regret that it should be wasted in town. For the autumn is a precious season. They call its days melancholy. Maybe they are, but they are delicious, and full of inspirations, not to be missed if one can help it. One does miss most of them in New York. Central Park in the spring is fairly responsive to the touch of nature. The grass grows, the leaves come out, there are lovely blossoms; the sights and smells of spring are strong enough to pervade the place in spite of its border of stone houses. And the little parks, too, with their formal flower-beds, have a real air of spring about them. But the charm of autumn is too subtle to be caught in parks. There are no flowers. The autumn smells are faint scents of dead leaves and of wet earth and of the pungent smoke from brush-heaps. There is smoke enough in town from the boiling asphalt and hoisting engines and oil-refineries and the like, but it hasn't much autumnal quality. One wants leaves underfoot in October, and the color of the dying foliage. Central Park has little of either. The dying foliage there merely gets dirty and drops, and is carted off. The Park is better than the streets, but it is not good enough. The bigger and simpler parks in the Bronx are much more like the real country, but they are not in town.

Arthur Finch had spent most of the summer in town, where hospital duties, highly prized by beginning doctors, had kept him busy. He was freer now that his older brethren were getting back from their vacations, and it took no parental urging to bring from him a prompt "Yes,

thank you!" in response to Mrs. Herron's note.
He picked up Mr. Herron on the ferry-boat.
They read the papers together on the train, and
got out at Antwerp in time to have daylight for
their drive from the station to the house. They
had a cup of tea, with the pleasant, desultory
discourse that timely tea invites. They dressed,
they dined; they played two or three rubbers
of bridge. It was an easy, pleasant, well-
ordered household, its members on good terms
with one another, the cook, and the world.
Arthur liked it, and his spirit, a little jaded by
a good deal of anxious work, took kindly to
repose. Mrs. Herron called him by his first
name, and upbraided him when his makes were
bad or his cards poor.

The next morning Susan took him to ride.
"How much of a horseman are you, Dr. Finch?"
she asked him.

"I try to continue with the horse when he
is going my way," he said. "I don't know that
I can say much more than that."

"But I think you have been on a horse before."

71

The Courtship of a Careful Man

"Oh yes."

"If that horse you are on now wanted to jump a fence, would you let him?"

"I think so, if it was not too high, and he seemed bent on it, and you assured me that he could do it, and the other side of the fence looked hospitable."

"Oh, he can do it, and, having an ardent nature, he will want to do anything he sees my mare do, and she is quite likely to jump a fence or two when the fields invite on a fine morning like this. But if you prefer to keep to the road, we will keep to the road."

"Not at all; I am of an aspiring nature myself, though timid; and, though an ignorant horseman, I am not entirely unpractised. I like very well to go across country when the fences are not all wire. I suppose your mare doesn't jump wire fences, does she?"

"Not when I am on her. But are you really of an aspiring nature, and really timid? And isn't that rather a painful conflict of qualities?"

"Oh no; not to hurt. It only means a balance

of faculties. Aspiration makes for energy, and timidity for prudence. Folks who are not afraid have to cultivate prudence as a mental accomplishment. Timid persons like me get it by instinct, and can put so much more of their minds on the cultivation of the aggressive qualities."

"But timid people are afraid. You can't make me believe that it's nice to be afraid."

"I sha'n't try. It isn't nice to be afraid, though a brisk, lively apprehension is often timely. There is an extreme of physical timidity which is a great misfortune. But the ordinary, governable timidity of an educated and disciplined person isn't so bad. It only means that he has to ride himself with spurs sometimes instead of a curb."

"Ride himself!"

"Yes; don't you think so?"

"I am not used to splitting myself in two like that."

"It's only a figure of speech. You compel yourself and control yourself, don't you?"

"When I want to do anything I do it, if I

73

can; and when I don't want to do anything I don't do it, if I can help it."

"What a nice, simple, direct nature! What fun you must have living!"

"Don't you?"

"I have enough; most of it in small ways. Work is pretty interesting—at least mine is getting to be so. Success is pleasant even in small things."

"What do you mean by success?"

"Oh — doing things right and getting good results."

"I think you must like doctoring."

"It isn't bad if you can learn how, and don't blunder too much, and don't have to make too much money at it."

"What heresy! Don't you want to make money?"

"Oh, I don't mind, but I don't want to have to make very much very soon. That's slavery. But I sha'n't have to make very much for a long time to come, please Heaven."

"I think you are a very odd person, you have such queer views. When will you be fifty?"

The Making of a Match

"Along about 1925, if I am there. But why queer?"

"Don't you know that society is divided into people who have money enough and want more, and people who haven't enough and want as much as possible as soon as possible? Where do you come in?"

"I don't come in yet. I am a bachelor."

"And do you think that it is getting married that makes men so greedy?"

"They have to be greedy, poor things, if they are married, unless they have independent fortunes."

"I have heard of bachelors who seemed fairly greedy. I have even known of cases where it was thought that men got married because they were disinclined to provide themselves with an independent maintenance."

"I dare say that happens sometimes, though it never seemed to me an astute proceeding to marry money for the sake of money and give yourself in part payment."

"I hope you won't do that."

"A timid nature like mine naturally shrinks
6 75

from such perils. I trust that you also will avoid them."

"I certainly shall try. Do you see that snake-fence?"

"Isn't it pretty! And that panel yonder has a rotten top rail and good landing beyond, which appeals to my timidity."

"Come on, then! . . . Well, we got over. Did he take it kindly?"

"Like a bird. Bless the horse!"

"Let us keep to the fields awhile. We can bear over towards the left there and through the woods, and strike the road again two or three miles back. Where the fences are too formidable there are always gates. I love the smell of the autumn woods when the leaves are falling. Don't you? And, oh, it's good to get off the beaten track and pick one's own way and overcome one's own obstacles. There's a bit too much of the beaten track in civilized life, don't you think? There is in a woman's life, anyway."

"There is in a man's life, too. That's one of the penalties of civilization. The compensa-

76

tion is that faster progress is possible along the beaten track than where you shape your own course and break your own road."

"Oh, progress! Yes, of a certain sort, no doubt. But I get tired of cut-and-dried progress. The women get all the cut-and-dried part, and, if there is any progress, the men get it. What kind of progress is possible for a girl with indulgent parents who provide for all her needs?"

"Well, there is always the possibility of discovering more wants and trying to satisfy them. That seems to be the chief thing we human creatures are here for. It isn't what the catechism suggests as the chief end of man, but it is the most obvious process by which civilization advances. The whole business of civilization is a development of fresh needs and a scramble to supply them. Can't you think of any new wants?"

"What a wise young doctor! What about that fence ahead?"

"I see a gate."

"I don't need a gate yet. I have developed a want of excitement."

The Courtship of a Careful Man

"Oh, well, there's a good place—the fourth panel from the gate. I'll give you a lead this time."

"That was nice. This really does me good. That fence was pretty well up to four feet, but you cracked the top rail for me. Do you know, I don't think you are so timid as you make out."

"Oh yes, I am. You forget that this is your father's horse, and that your father's daughter was looking on. Put me off by myself, make me responsible for the legs of a borrowed horse, and take away the inspiration of being under your eye, and you would see all my natural timidity assert itself. It makes a difference— Hello! What was that? It sounded like a horn. There again—*toot, toot, toot!* Have you got a hunt in this country?"

"Sometimes the Anniston hounds work down this way."

"That must be it. Let's have a look. Come through yonder, where the fence is broken. There's the pack, sure enough, and feathering for all they are worth. Bless me, isn't that pretty! Do you see the huntsman? The field must be beyond the wood. Those hounds must think they've got something. Why, this is too good to believe. There they go; hear them! Why, they must be after a fox! *I see him! I see him!* Look yonder on the hill-side. Come on. We need a little of this ourselves. Gracious, what luck!"

On they galloped, both horses eager, over fence, field, ploughed land, and highway, crossing a railroad, guided through woods by the cry of the hounds, dodging down a ravine and up the other side, keeping the huntsman as well in sight as possible, and profiting as much as they might by his judgment. When he skirted a wire fence they followed him, and got through where he got through. When he broke a rail or a board they steered for the gap. Having by luck the start of the field, they had clear going, and the few riders who came up by superior speed were some distance away and did not bother them. Five miles of it, with hardly a check, brought them up to a baffled pack clamoring for a fox that had gone to earth. The master of the hounds rode up to them.

The Courtship of a Careful Man

"The Anniston Hounds are honored by Miss Herron's company," he said. "I am sorry I have no brush to offer her. How does it happen that I have never seen her out before?"

"My father hasn't encouraged me to hunt, Mr. Felton, but I was showing Dr. Finch the country—I beg to present Dr. Finch—and we stumbled on the hounds by accident, and they ran away with him, and I had to follow or go home alone."

"Very glad it happened so. I will send you a list of the meets, and it may happen so again. Very glad to meet Dr. Finch, too, and I hope to see him again."

"But I didn't know you hunted wild foxes hereabout," said Arthur.

"Ordinarily we don't, but a fox turns up now and then when we can get an early start," and the master smiled.

"How far are we from Antwerp station, Mr. Felton?" Susan asked.

"Oh, ten or twelve miles; but don't go home."

"What does Dr. Finch say?"

"Dr. Finch surmises that a five-mile run is

The Making of a Match

probably enough for horses that are hardly in hunting training."

"And twelve miles still to go. I dare say Dr. Finch is right. Thank you for so much good sport, Mr. Felton, and please start us in the right direction."

"Down that road a couple of miles. Take the first turn to the right, and keep on till you strike your own neighborhood. Good-bye."

"Well," said Arthur, as they rode away, "we got in touch with the strenuous life for nearly an hour. It does one good when it comes his way, though I have never had much spunk about going out and looking for it. Wasn't it luck to have caught on to those hounds!"

"Wonderful!" But Susan's eyes twinkled as she said so. He looked back at her suspiciously.

"I shouldn't wonder if it was a put-up job. Please, did you know those hounds were coming down here to-day?"

"I thought they might. The meet was at Hebron, and last year when they met there they came down through those fields where we saw them first. I happened on them there last year, that's the truth, and I thought we might happen on them again."

"What a thoughtful, considerate lady! Did you get a run last year?"

"No! I had Alfred Dyckman with me, and I didn't dare take him. I knew he would fall off, and I was afraid he would break his neck, and people would say I did it on purpose."

"You seemed to have no fears about me."

"Oh no; you ride better than he does; really, you ride pretty well. And, besides, if you had broken your neck, it would have been just an accident."

"Whereas Mr. Dyckman—"

"Oh, if it had happened to him, mother would certainly have charged me with homicide."

"Why?"

"Well, he was so troublesome. He's rather troublesome, anyway, and he was particularly troublesome about that time. It is quite different with you."

"We're not alike, then?"

"Not a bit. He's more timid than you in some respects, and less so—possibly—in others.

82

The Making of a Match

And he was more civilized than you, in that he had developed lots more wants. He was eager to make more money, and his mind ran on stocks, and—oh, well, he wanted the earth generally. Perhaps you know him."

"I have met him, but hardly more than that. I don't know him well enough to have found out that he was troublesome. You see, I have been away from home a good deal until this last summer. If he is so troublesome, I don't want to know him."

"Oh, I dare say he'd never trouble you a mite. No doubt he has his uses, and I can even imagine a person finding a use for him. But not I. I was never able to develop a want—as you would say—that he could meet. But that's no particular discredit to him. It's the trouble with men generally; they seem so much more disposed, and so much better qualified, to develop wants than to supply them. Here's our road to the right. I've got some sandwiches in this saddle-box. Have one? I thought there was a chance of our being late in getting back."

"Thank you. You are a kind lady to me

this day, but about men in general you seem less kind, and I dare say that by to-morrow you will have lumped me in with all the rest."

"I'm not sure. You see, you seem to me peculiar in some respects. Aren't you a little less greedy than the others? You said you didn't want to make money, and you intimated —I understood it so—that you were not bent on marrying any one, and—well, I got the impression that you were resigned to your lot in life, and I had begun to think that you might possibly be a useful subject for observation."

"Who can tell? The humblest of God's creatures in its humblest operations may yield lessons of supreme wisdom to the inquiring eye that has learned to see."

Late on Sunday afternoon, when Arthur Finch went back to town, Susan took him to the station in a light wagon.

"Thank you," he said, "for two happy days. Are you coming back to town soon?"

"As soon as the days grow so short that father can't read the newspapers on the train coming out, and the frost has killed the flowers in mother's garden, and the roads are too muddy for me to ride over."

"And that will be—?"

"Sometime between Election Day and Thanksgiving, according to the season. If the weather holds good, and the town gets tiresome, come back to us. If mother doesn't invite you, telephone out and invite yourself. If you come early enough on Saturday, I'll take you to ride again, or you can golf with father."

When she got back to the house her mother stood waiting, with her hat on.

"Take me out for a little air, Susan." She got in. "My young man seemed to like his visit. I thank you for your polite toleration of him. I hope he didn't bore you?"

"No, mother. He wasn't very tiresome. I even asked him to come again. I think your taste in young men is improving."

"My luck may be improving; but I had not seen Arthur Finch for years, so it wasn't a case of better judgment. He played good bridge, I thought."

The Courtship of a Careful Man

"Then you will let him come again if he asks. I told him he might ask. I thought he was a nice, safe man. He took his fences well yesterday."

"You ought not to have gone after those hounds. I wish you would not do such things; but if you must, it is a relief to have a doctor along. I am told that Arthur takes his work seriously, and is thought to be promising."

"I wonder if he is really good at it. I think he picked up a patient yesterday. Coming home, we passed the Macks' cottage, and Annie Mack was walking about the barn-yard, her poor little legs jerking sixteen ways at once at every step. It just makes me cry to see that child. He got off his horse, found Mack in the barn, talked with him and asked him some questions, and then he caught Annie and took her in his lap and felt all of her poor little bones. I told him that if he would straighten up Annie's legs I'd give him the best Boston-terrier puppy in our next litter."

"Susan!"

"He said Annie's legs seemed to have been

The Making of a Match

struck by lightning, but that he had seen surgeons in Europe who could do remarkable things
with them, and there were men in New York
who could better them at least. He is going
to find out about it, and possibly I am to borrow Annie and have her brought to town. It
breaks my heart to think of that child strug-
gling through life on those legs. They have
haunted me ever since I first saw her."

"See, Susan! There's an automobile coming. Do be careful. I'd like to get out."

"Sit tight, mother! There's no ditch here.
Steady there, Jonathan! There! He doesn't
mind them any more; but really those automobile people have no manners. They ought not
to be allowed to go out of sight of the police."

It was early in January that Mr. and Mrs.
Herron dined at the Rakoffs', and Judge Finch
took Mrs. Herron out to dinner.

"I had a glimpse of your promising young
son at our house yesterday, judge."

"Did you? No sickness in your family, I
hope."

"Not yesterday; but he lanced a felon for my cook last week, and I am going to have him in to vaccinate a new maid as soon as I can remember it. He seems to be acquiring a practice."

"I hope so. And yesterday—?"

"Yesterday he was just taking a cup of tea."

"And exchanging conversation, no doubt, with your dangerous and difficult young daughter. And how is your dangerous young daughter, Mrs. Herron? Do you know, my wife is liable to question you at any time about her intentions. She begins to be uneasy. There! She is looking at us now— A glass of wine with you, Mrs. Finch! She says the Herrons see more of Arthur this winter than she does, and she has intimated to me—I beg your pardon—that Miss Susan Herron has rather an alarming reputation as a flirt."

"Poor Susan! The most kind-hearted girl in the world. I trust you told Mrs. Finch that the whole responsibility of Arthur's acquaintance with Susan rested on you."

"No, I didn't! My professional experience

88

long ago broke me of the habit of making impulsive admissions. Confession may be good for the soul, but it deranges the orderly procedure of justice. People are so apt, in the enthusiasm of divulging news, to confess more than really happened."

"But, judge, it *was* all your suggestion."

"Was it, really? I don't think I shall remember until I see how it's coming out. Meanwhile I trust my promising young son is not causing your daughter's parents any uneasiness, and that Susan has not yet asked to be taken abroad."

"Not yet, but the season is young still. Susan can't leave town yet, anyway. She has a patient in a hospital. Did Arthur tell you about little Annie Mack?"

"Little Annie Mack? Not that I remember."

"Annie lives out our way, and her means of locomotion are very much impaired, and Susan has had her brought in town to a hospital, and—"

"Oh, she must be the child with the fantastic

legs that Arthur told us about. She has been
his pet patient for a month past. He makes
his mother buy dolls for her. Has he got Miss
Susan interested in her, too?"

"I don't know whether it was he who got her
interested, or she him, but Annie is certainly
very much on Susan's mind."

"He didn't say he had an accomplice."

"A case of hereditary reticence, maybe."

"Possibly. After all, it's a good quality in a
doctor. You don't think it is my duty to warn
his mother, do you?"

"And risk impairing Susan's confidence in
her mother's discretion? It is not for me to
urge any man to keep anything from his wife,
but are you sure it would be news to Mrs.
Finch? I have known of cases where mothers
knew more about their son's doings than fathers
did. My boy in college tells me everything."

"I dare say. I was once a boy in college,
and I have since had a boy in college, and I
know that college - boys are remarkably com-
municative, and tell their mothers everything
that they think their mother's experience of

life qualifies them to appreciate. I dare say it is so with young doctors, too, and that what, if anything, they see fit not to disclose is withheld out of filial regard for their mother's peace of mind."

"Judge, you give yourself airs. That is not quite the sort of discourse which a mother finds reassuring."

"It need not worry you. I was only following up your suggestion that discretion ought to be used about forcing information upon mothers which their sons may not have seen fit to impart to them. The best that can be done for boys is to qualify them to take care of themselves, and we all know that taking good care of one's self involves, first or last, a fair capacity for keeping one's own counsel."

Late in March, Arthur Finch came home and found his mother with a little dog asleep in her lap. "Why, mother," he exclaimed, "where did you get that dog? Who ever could have expected to see my careful mother develop a fancy for dogs?"

The Courtship of a Careful Man

"She hasn't. This is not my dog. It is yours. A man brought it in this basket, and left this note addressed to you, which, being unsealed, I have read, and am not much the wiser."

"Let's see! 'For Dr. Finch; on account of a grateful patient.' I haven't any grateful patients."

"It came only half an hour ago. I had it put in the bath-room, and it cried, and because it was your dog I took it out of the basket. But I could not let it run around, and it went to sleep in my lap."

"What is it like? It's a Boston terrier. Very fashionable little dog, mother. Who ever sent me a Boston— Oh! That child with the twisted legs that I am looking after has a friend that raises Boston terriers. Annie's legs are none too good yet—a dachshund would have been more appropriate—but I am glad of any sign that her friends like the way the job is going!"

"Are you going to keep him?"

"You wouldn't part a doctor from his fee, would you?"

The Making of a Match

"I'm glad it isn't a Newfoundland. I had
not thought of boarding a dog; but having a
doctor in the house is a convenience, and we
must put up with its incidents."

When the courts closed for the summer,
Judge and Mrs. Finch went abroad. The Herron family spent the early summer at Antwerp,
and when Antwerp grew too hot for entire comfort, Susan and her mother migrated to Pemaquid Bay, in Maine.

"PEMAQUID BAY, MAINE, *August* 1, 19—.

"MY DEAR DR. FINCH,—Can you sail a boat? Our
sailorman can, but I have pretty much used up his
conversation. If you can sail a boat, there is a good
opening here for a person of your qualifications; and
if not, our sailorman and I could teach you, and it is a
good place to learn. Father is here, and thinks pretty
well of the golf-links. Mother would play bridge six
hours a day instead of five, as at present, if she had
your help. My brother William approves of our environment, and says there is 'a remarkably good line
of girls hereabouts.' He is young still, as you know,
and so are most of the girls; but in girls—as you know
—youth is an excusable defect. The air here is salu-
brious, and is highly recommended by physicians to
persons who have spent the month of July in town.

The Courtship of a Careful Man

Mother sends you her compliments, and directs me
to offer you the simple hospitalities of her cottage,
beginning when you arrive, and lasting during your
honorable pleasure   Yours sincerely,
                                "Susan Herron."

The issue of this letter was the appearance
of Dr. Arthur Finch at Pemaquid Bay on August 8th.   Three weeks later he held the tiller of
the sail-boat *Glint,* under orders of Miss Susan
Herron, skipper.

"I was thinking that before I went back I
would ask you to marry me, and this is my last
day!"

"Keep her off a little; the jib's flapping.   I
beg your pardon.   What were you saying?"

"Only that I was thinking that before I went
back I would ask you to marry me, and that
this was my last day!"

"Oh! Well, I — I'm glad you haven't.
Father says he never sets himself any vacation
tasks; it spoils his fun.   I think that's a good
rule.   I was going to read a lot of Herbert
Spencer—the jib isn't pulling a mite—while I
was up here, and I brought the books along;

"UNDER ORDERS OF MISS SUSAN HERRON, SKIPPER"

but I haven't opened them. The next best thing to not intending to do anything in August is not to do what you intend."

"Of course that is a sound general sentiment, but with Herbert Wilson on his way up from Marblehead on a schooner-yacht, it doesn't seem to me as timely as it might."

"He's got the wind dead ahead, what there is of it."

"It won't stay so, and as I was saying—"

"Really, you must pay attention to sailing this boat, unless you mean to let her gybe with the sheet two-thirds out."

"You are absolutely discouraging."

"I don't mean to turn a man from the path of duty if his feet are obstinately set in it, but it is such a nice sailing-day!"

"*Duty?* Misery! *Duty?*"

"Why dissemble? What other motive could excuse such a suggestion in a man of declared sentiments such as yours? An ordinary, troublesome man might have an ordinary motive, but not you! She's falling off again."

"Oh, let her drop! What have you laid up

against me? What sentiments have I ever declared?"

"You shake my faith in mankind—you that were a bachelor and did not have to be greedy, and hoped not to be for years to come. And I have thought of you as a safe person, and confided in you with all the credulity of inexperience—"

"Inexperience! Oh, dear!"

"—of inexperience, and played with you as confidently as—as—"

"I respect your hesitation. It becomes you."

"And I had thought you sincere, and you turn out to be merely plausible. There's a puff of wind coming. Do you see?"

"I didn't bind myself never to progress. That was almost a whole year ago. I had just begun to know you then. All my professions were suitable for a man who had met you only the day before, and had learned of you chiefly as a dangerous young woman. I told you that civilization was a process of developing wants. Am I to be shut off from the privileges of a civilized—"

The Making of a Match

"Excuse me! If you don't come about, we shall be on the rocks. If you will pull in the sheet, I will look after the jib. There! You were arguing—?"

"Arguing nothing; merely asserting my privilege as a civilized man to develop a want in the course of a year."

"In the course of a year! What deliberation!"

"You know better. A woman of your experience must have recognized that it was virtually at first sight."

"Only virtually? And you want to go and risk the last of your summer holidays on a mere virtuality!"

"Well, I will speak to your father as soon as we get ashore."

"You won't make the landing unless you keep her up better. What are you going to say to father?"

"I am going to ask his consent to my marrying you."

"You haven't got mine yet."

"Please come and take the tiller for a moment."

The Courtship of a Careful Man

"No, I don't think I will. Our sailorman is watching you from the wharf, and he expects you to do credit to his lessons."

"Then I may speak to him?"

"Not a word to the sailorman, nor even to father. Let my dear father have his holiday out. Neither he nor I can bear to be pestered with hard questions in August."

"But you are coming home in a fortnight."

"And meanwhile you will have a chance to remember how disadvantageous it is to a beginning doctor to have to concern himself about money-making."

"And you will have a chance to consider Herbert Wilson, whose money is all made."

"Herbert Wilson isn't going to be troublesome. Bring her up without bumping her, and you shall have a long mark!"

"That isn't just what I want at this moment. What shall I do for a whole fortnight, until you come home?"

"Have patience, and grope along, and, if necessary, write to me. What is a mere fortnight among two?"

The Making of a Match

"Among *two!* It is not much among two. All ready to come about! Mind the boom! Catch her, Johnson! Thank you! That was beautiful. Please, lady, give me my long mark!"

The wedding came after Easter. When the bride and groom had gone away, Judge Finch, with two glasses of champagne, sought out Mrs. Herron.

"I bring a cup of consolation to the mother of the bride."

"I think, judge, that you must feel that you invented this wedding."

"Marriages are made in heaven. I trust that this one was. We have not hindered it, certainly, but here's hoping that it may turn out to be far better devised than either you or I could have planned."

They drank the wine. Mrs. Herron wiped her eyes; the judge snuffled a little. They both smiled.

"Well, judge, it was a sweet wedding, wasn't it?"

A Disguised Providence

A Disguised Providence

OU will be interested to know, sir, that I am engaged."

"Engaged to be married?"

"That was the understanding."

"Why, Henry!"

"Why not, father?"

"You haven't got my consent, for one thing, and—my boy, what are you getting engaged on?"

"I supposed it would strike you as rather speculative."

"Rather."

"But, after all, I am twenty-seven years old."

"Oh no, Henry; twenty-seven years young. Twenty-seven years impecunious; twenty-seven years rash and improvident!"

The Courtship of a Careful Man

"And I am a practising lawyer, with my name on an office door, a fourth interest in a stenographer, and some clients."

"Clients! *Quorum pars maxima fui.*"

"And an allowance made me by my father, who is a generous man, though not rich."

"An old, precarious man who works for his living, and has a wife to provide for. A reed shaken regularly by the wind every spring, and driven to Lakewood and sometimes to Florida. A poor, propped-up ruin, liable to fall in any day, and not over-well insured. A doting parent, of course, and yet one whose allowances may not safely be regarded as perpetual annuities. Allowances should be made for the young, Henry. Allowances must often be made for engaged persons; but, Lord! Henry, what are you going to marry on?"

"Now, father, don't take it so hard. I'll bet I could scrape along if you turned me loose. I took in nearly a hundred dollars last month, and it is less than two years since I began practice. Besides, I only said I was engaged; I'm not married yet. You'll see it in

A Disguised Providence

the papers when I'm married, so be easy. It
is not such a terrible expense to be engaged,
though, if you have a mind to make some tem-
porary enlargement of my resources, I can use
the money."

"I have no doubt, if you really are engaged,
that you've run in debt somewhere for a ring."

"Not yet, but I'm going to. I haven't got
your consent yet."

"Have you told your mother?"

"I thought I would first give you an opportunity to consent of your own free will. Besides, mother is an observant person, and goes
out a good deal between breakfast and dinner,
and reads the papers, and it is hard to surprise
her with news."

"By thunder! Henry, I believe you really
are engaged."

"Aren't you ever going to ask me who is
the girl?"

"Of course, if it is so, it's some nice girl. I
hadn't got to the girl. A mind stunned by a
general proposition must clear before it can
grasp details. Twenty-seven years young, be-

longs to one or two clubs, has a fair collection of outstanding bills, has an allowance from an impaired father, earned nearly a hundred dollars last month, and is engaged to be married, and expects to owe for a ring! Well, Henry, who *is* the fortunate lady?"

"Jane Templeton is the lady, sir."

"Jane Templeton! Jane Templeton! I seem to know the name. I've seen Jane Templeton somewhere, haven't I?"

"Don't you remember a dinner we had here last month?"

"Yes; that's it. A juvenile dinner, that you got up, and you let your mother and me come to the table, and your mother thought it was so considerate of you. Now Jane was there, wasn't she? And she sat— Where did she sit, Henry?"

"Why, father, she sat on your right!"

"Lord bless me! so she did; so she did! And that's the girl. Dark hair and light-blue eyes. Extraordinarily nice eyes. I don't notice the color of eyes once a year. Why, that's a dear girl, Henry. Let's see! She was going to the

A Disguised Providence

opera, and she talked about Corots, and scarabæi, and old tapestries, and yachts, and Newport, and dahabeeyahs, and hospitals, and slum settlements, and expensive subjects of that sort; and she had on— What did she have on? Somehow I only remember how lovely she looked, and that I thought so, and that I was thankful I wasn't supporting her. Why, Henry, what bait did you use? Jane Templeton! Who's her father? Has she no mother, no friends? What did you tell him?"

"Her father was James Templeton, of Templeton & Condit. You know the firm. He's dead. He worked too hard. Her mother's dead, too. I blush to say that Jane is an orphan, and an only child, and lives with her aunt."

"James Templeton's only child! You have imposed upon that young woman. She must have a very respectable fortune. Has her aunt no control over her? Has she no guardian?"

"Why, dear father, what ails her? It isn't only that I am going to get *her*. She is going to get *me*. She's doing well. The aunt doesn't greatly mind, and, for that matter, doesn't greatly count, though she is a competent aunt and a good lady. The guardian's responsibility ceased two years ago. There is a trustee; that's all. There probably is a good deal of money, but I can't help it."

"I suppose not. You'll just have to live it down. But I had not at all foreseen such an accident, and you must excuse me if I feel the shock. The gold-brick stratagem is nothing to it. What do you think she sees in you, Henry?"

"My dear dad's likeness, I dare say. She as good as said so the night she dined here."

"A fortune and a sweet gift of speech. Maybe I shall get a daughter out of this—let alone grandchildren. We must make the best of it, but it grieves me to think how much better she might have done!"

"No such thing, father. Of course there has been a squad of willing souls that she might have had, but—oh—some were too fat, and some too rich, and some too old, and some incapable of domestication, and most of them had impediments of one kind or another, and I

108

really couldn't see where she could do much better. And besides, I told her that if she took me she would get the best father-in-law in town, and the most sympathetic mother-in-law; and that settled it."

"You are a very smooth young man, Henry. You have imposed on that nice girl. But if you are really going to marry into affluence, I am going to take your mother up the Nile next winter. I have put by nearly enough for her and me, and why shouldn't we enjoy life? Perhaps your Jane will give me a cup of tea about five o'clock to-morrow? Yes? I naturally wish to pay my respects to so altruistic a lady. Meet me there? No, thank you! If you will just say I'm coming, that will be all."

"She has nice hands, Henry; good, strong, competent hands."

"I understood that you held one of them."

"I dare say. Her mind seemed fairly composed so far as you were concerned."

"I looked in myself at six, and was glad to

find you had not unsettled it. Did you congratulate her?"

"I didn't seem to find words for that, knowing you as I do, but I welcomed her. I had no trouble about that."

"She said you seemed hospitably inclined towards her. Did you ask for a settlement?"

"No; you'll have to send your solicitor if you want a settlement. I don't think she is over-well posted on fiscal concerns, anyway. Nothing that I said about the market seemed to take hold at all. She got so far once as to say, 'Mr. Pelton says so and so.' Who's Mr. Pelton?"

"He's Samuel Pelton, who succeeded his father as trustee of her father's estate. You've met him, haven't you?"

"I don't remember him. The old man was an upright, conservative old party. Now you speak of it, it seems to me that there was some gossip about the son being caught in the May panic, and rather hard hit. If that's so, I trust he lost his own money. I dare say, Henry, you may get some business out of that estate."

"In time, no doubt. Meanwhile the proposi-

110

A Disguised Providence

tion is for a wedding after Easter, and a few
months abroad."

"And leave a teething law practice in charge
of a trained nurse, I suppose. By George!
Henry, that 'll be mighty inconvenient for you,
and not over-timely for me. Well, you can sell
the bonds your grandfather left you. The wash
of these ample fortunes is very upsetting to
small craft. We have sat on those poor old
bonds, or their predecessors, ever since you
were a baby, and over they go in a bread-cast-
upon-the-waters investment that smacks a little too much of pleasure to be business and a
little too much of business to be perfect pleasure. But then, no pleasure is perfect. It's
terribly like false pretences and bunco, but I
suppose the end justifies the means."

"If you really think—"

"I don't really think. I'm not going to
think, I'm not going to meddle, I'm not even
going to croak any more. I threw away your
leading-strings five years ago. That nice girl
seems to have rather too much money; much
more than you are used to; rather more, I judge,

The Courtship of a Careful Man

than she is used to yet, for she has barely come into it. But life is full of perils, and as between the anxieties of dearth, and the hazards of super-abundance, I suppose we all prefer to take our chances with superfluity."

A month later. The same to the same.

"Well, father! Have you read the evening papers?"

"Not the late editions. I saw the six-o'clock edition of something about noon, but it had no news in it. Anything up?"

"A good deal. Most interesting. Sam Pelton's killed!"

"Pelton? So? Our Jane's trustee?"

"Just that."

"Run over by an automobile?"

"No; safe at home in his own apartment at the Pelion, just after noon. They're digging a cellar across the street, and the noon blast sent a five-ton chunk of rock through Pelton's window and caught him as he stood before the window shaving. Poor man! it made a pancake of him."

A Disguised Providence

"Shocking! Why, Henry, the perils of this town are awful. Folks who value their lives will soon be hiring cells in bomb-proof lodging-houses. How did Pelton come to be dressing so late in the morning? Doesn't he go to his office?"

"I don't know. Up late last night, maybe; or perhaps he wasn't well. Anyhow, he's done for, poor chap. He had no partner, and as Jane's concerns were altogether in his hands, I dare say it will be an interesting job to transfer them. She is much shocked, naturally."

"What's to be done?"

"That is what she has been asking me. Of course there will have to be an accounting by Pelton's estate, and a transfer of the trust, which has a number of years to run yet. I told her she ought to have first-rate advice at once, and we telephoned over to Judge Holly, and he is coming to see her to-night."

"She knows the judge, does she?"

"Oh yes; she has always known him. He knew her father. I'm going over there to dinner."

The Courtship of a Careful Man

"My gracious! Think of that unlucky Pelton flattened out so in his own bedroom. Henry, if you will go out, go carefully. Don't fall into the subway; avoid cabs—you can't afford them, and they're dangerous, anyhow; keep your weather-eye out for automobiles. It's a couple of days since they killed any one, and they must be hungry. If you must ride in the street-cars, sit as near the door as you can without getting in the draught. I saw a street-car burn clean up on the track this afternoon. They had to get the fire department out and play on it; a most curious and highly scandalous sight. Still, the street-cars with all their risks are safer than the other vehicles, for the company pays for what it runs over. Remember that you are an only son, and the affianced of an orphan whose trustee is dead, and step gingerly."

The fifth week in lent.

"You're quite a stranger, Henry. You've dined out every night this week. I only see you at breakfast, and a man isn't much com-

A Disguised Providence

fort at breakfast. I wish I had raised some girls, but I always did wish that. Are you going out to-night, son?"

"I'm going over to dine with Jane. There are matters of moment to be discussed."

"No doubt, and your impending marriage only a fortnight off."

"Judge Holly sent for me this afternoon."

"And how was the judge?"

"A good deal flustered, and he had a good deal to say."

"Ah?"

"Yes; since his appointment a week ago as Jane's trustee in Pelton's place, he has been forgathering with Pelton's administrator, and they have got the seals off Pelton's books and various receptacles, and have been trying to find Jane's estate."

"Well, didn't Pelton keep his accounts straight?"

"Yes; there's plenty of accounts. His clerks did that. The accounts are satisfactory. The trouble is with the securities. They couldn't find them."

115

"Wasn't there a list of them?"

"Oh yes; they found the list. The list is splendid; most exemplary. But they haven't got the securities."

"Where did Pelton keep them?"

"He had a big safe-deposit box. They have found that and opened it. The box is safe, but it was empty."

"Had Pelton pledged them?"

"That's it. There were a lot of bonds that they haven't run down yet, but they have traced stocks enough through the transfer-books of various railways to get a pretty clear idea of what has happened. As trustee, Pelton had complete power. He evidently went into a big gamble in the spring, pledged a lot of Jane's papers, was caught in the May crush, and sold out. He bet what was left in an effort to get even, and the corn failure and the steel strike finished him. No wonder he kept away from his office! He was done. There is some real estate, and on that he has managed to raise enough to pay Jane her income. It was Heaven's mercy to him that that rock came through

116

his window before the bigger one that hung over him had time to drop."

"Is there nothing left?"

"Certainly nothing compared with what is gone. The judge says there is the house, and some other real estate that is valuable. None of it is clear, but the blast that cut Pelton off before he was quite ready seems to have saved Jane some equities and other remnants that are worth something."

"But you don't know what they are worth?"

"No; the tangle is too bad, the judge says, for any estimate to be worth anything yet. There is no record of what Pelton did. Some mortgages are recorded; there may be others that are not."

"Does Jane know it?"

"Not yet. The question is, who is to tell her, and when? Am I to tell her to-night? The invitations are out to her wedding. Must it be put off? The only thing I have done yet is to give up my steamer rooms. We can't go abroad, anyhow."

117

The Courtship of a Careful Man

"Henry, this is getting too complicated for you and me. Ask for some tea, and see if your mother has come in yet. I think I heard her. Here she is. Come, Fanny, and have some tea. Henry's got a tale. The bark that carries his hopes is aground, and seems stove in. We need help to get her off. Tell her, Henry."

"The short of it is, mother, that our Jane has gone broke, and doesn't know it yet. Her trustee had stolen pretty much all her fortune."

"Mercy!"

"And the question is, Fanny, whether the wedding can go on, and whether Jane shall be told this tale of disaster before or after it."

"Is it really true, Charles?"

"Strictly, absolutely true. At least, so Henry says."

"Then of course she must know it. She may not want Henry if she has lost her money."

"There, Henry; that's a consideration. Jane may feel that you are a luxury beyond her

118

A Disguised Providence

present means. She may feel constrained to marry a richer man now. You'll have to tell her. If you don't, Judge Holly will. He's bound to. But, Fanny, how about putting the wedding off?"

"That's for Jane to say. It's bad luck to put off weddings. I hope she won't. She's got her gown, and I've got mine, and I don't want to see either of them put away to get out of fashion. Then there are her presents."

"But, Fanny, Henry's only earning— How much was it last month, Henry?"

"A hundred and thirty, father, but really the practice is picking up."

"If Henry can't support her, Charles, you've got to. There's nothing the matter with Henry except that he's a beginner. Starting out to marry a poor girl on a very small income is one thing. This is a different case entirely. Jane is a dear girl, and will make the loveliest bride you ever saw. I'll share anything you've got with her."

"Very well, Fanny, but we won't be able to go up the Nile—not this year."

The Courtship of a Careful Man

"The Nile will keep. The frocks won't. Karnak will be just as good style ten years from now as it is to-day."

"How do, Henry? Good man to have come early. Come and see the new presents."

"More?"

"Oh yes, lots more to-day. Some beautiful ones."

"Where's the good aunt?"

"Not down yet. Here they are. Look at these topazes. Aren't they lovely?"

"Put them on. There, now they *are* lovely. Are they real?"

"Surely. Look who sent them!"

"With the love of the Jarvises, eh? Oh yes, I guess they're real. And you too, Jane. You are real, too—a real person, who won't vanish into thin air when the clock strikes twelve and the fairy palace crumbles?"

"I a real person? Yes, Henry. Why not? Henry! What's got into your voice? Let me look at you! Why did you say that?"

"Jane Hawkshaw, the detective and mind-

A Disguised Providence

reader! Look hard, Jane. Look deep. What do you see?"

"Nothing but what I love, dear. And yet— What's happened, Henry? Have you brought some news?"

"Yes!"

"And not good news?"

"No, not exactly. Disconcerting sort of news, but not killing. The late Pelton stole a lot of your money, dear Jane. That's my news. There may be some left, but I fear not very much. It looks just now as though he had made a pretty clean sweep."

"How do you know about it, Henry?"

"I got it from Judge Holly this afternoon. I dare say he'll be here soon himself; this evening, perhaps. He's very low-spirited over it."

"But I had my income up to a month ago. How could it all go at once?"

"The judge will tell you. I fear you won't get any more income from your own estate for some time to come. Have you got some money in the bank?"

The Courtship of a Careful Man

"Some; not a great deal. What does it all mean to me?"

"It means a great deal. It means being rather a poor woman instead of a rich one. It means living in a small house instead of a big one, thinking what you can afford instead of what you want, going without quantities of things you have been used to having. It means all sorts of superficial changes, and it makes a poor man a worse match for you than he was before."

"But that's not all, Henry. That's not all!"

"That's enough. We can't unpack the whole of Pandora's box before dinner."

"Yes, but, Henry. It makes me a much worse match for a poor man than I was before."

"Do you think you can do better, Jane?"

"I am sure you could do better, Henry!"

"Oh, you flatter me. I don't think it. Who'd have me but you? Who'd take me second-hand? And if any one would have me, do you think I'm going to let the labor of years come to nothing, and go to work and court some new

A Disguised Providence

girl? Money's handy, dear Jane, but no particular lot of it is essential."

"N-no, Henry. But I had planned such
pleasant uses for it, and I had hoped to do so
many things for you. Besides, dear Henry,
what are we to live on?"

"I hope there'll be salvage enough from your
wreck to keep you from want, but, anyhow, it's
for me to find means of support for both of us,
and I have found them already."

"Where, Henry?"

"Chiefly at home, in the second-story front
room, sitting in front of a wood fire, taking tea
with mother. Also, in an office down-town."

"Your father!"

"Yes, Jane. Father and I. As for father,
dear man, he's used to it. He has supported
most of me these many years. Don't pity him.
He likes it. It won't be for long, for I expect
to be a prodigious wage-earner right away.
Mother says, 'Oh, don't put off the wedding!'
Cheer up, Jane. Set a storm-sail and head for
port. And oh, don't throw me over! After
all the ballast you've lost you can't spare an-

9   123

other pound; and oh, dear Jane, I would hate
it so!"

"You absurd Henry, you make me laugh.
Here comes Aunt Felicia. Don't tell her yet.
And here's William to say dinner's ready.
William, please send word to Judge Holly
that if he can come in this evening I should
like to see him. And say Mr. Warden is
here."

Ten days later.

"How goes the inquest, Henry?"

"Pretty well, father. There's going to be
something left."

"Wasn't Pelton quite thorough?"

"Oh, he did his best. The quick assets are
cleaned out absolutely. Everything that had
gilt on its edge is gone, but, as I told you, there
are some equities, and we have found a boxful
of the old man's bad investments that Pelton
never meddled with much. There's a collection
of deeds to Western and Southern lands in half
a dozen different states that must have looked
like waste paper ten years ago, but the judge

thinks they make interesting reading now. Father, I'm going to move my office!"

"So?"

"Yes; the judge says Jane's matters are going to be a long job, and that anyway there's room on his office door for another name, and that mine will look as well there as anywhere else."

"Great news! You'll get your office rent paid, anyhow."

"Much better than that. He was able to demonstrate that there is several times as much present income waiting for me in his office as I have been able to find so far in my own, and he talked hopefully about the future. He is a very pretty speaker, the judge is, when he has a mind to talk."

"There's no better office in town. You'll make a living yet. It's no very great trick for a well-equipped man, if you once get started. A little knowledge, a little talent, a little gumption, all the character you've got, and a day's work every day. The rest is a matter of opportunity, and that comes."

The Courtship of a Careful Man

And so they were married, and the wedding was no less lively than weddings ought to be, and the newspapers told all about it, and, as usual, somewhat more; and some of them, distressing but inevitable to tell, printed the bride's picture, besides making generous estimates of the value of the gifts. Every one knew that the bride was no longer an heiress of distinction, and everybody talked about it in private and ignored it in public. Everybody sympathized with her, and some persons pitied her, but many who were quite ready with pity, and even carried a supply of it with them to the wedding, were constrained to the conclusion that they had brought it to the wrong market. Somehow it wasn't that kind of a wedding, for, though it was fairly tearful at the church, and a good many women made furtive dabs with their handkerchiefs at their eyes and noses, and some elderly gentlemen snuffled, Major Brace, who was present, declared that he never was at a wedding which was less qualified by misgivings, or where the atmosphere was so heavily charged with affection and good-will. "We sunk the shop

"'WHAT'S THE USE OF HAVING AN ONLY SON IF YOU CAN'T SPOIL HIM?'"

A Disguised Providence

for the whole of two hours," said the major. "It was like real old times," and the intrepid man snuffled again and called for a cocktail, though it was barely five o'clock.

"Well, Charles, do you still expect to see the pyramids?"

"Give me time, Fanny, a little time. I'm not sixty yet, and there's lots of work in me. We'll see the pyramids at our leisure. Let them wait. I'd rather see my grandchildren than the pyramids any day. I'm glad you didn't put that wedding off. What's the use of having an only son if you can't spoil him?"

Josephine

Josephine

HERE is uneasiness in my mind about Josephine because she has no job. She is rising twenty-five, sound —reasonably sound—I have seen girls who ate up their breakfast better—combines dark hair with Saxon eyes, is kind, gentle, and well broken, goes remarkably well in single harness, and is not afraid of the cars nor much afraid of automobiles. I don't think she is enough afraid of autos. She has been out with young Kimberly in his, and also with the Blakes, and is beginning to concern herself about automobile millinery, which is a vanity, and prone to develop into grave expenditure. Besides, I don't seem to care especially for Kimberly, and her divaga-

131

tions with the Blakes simply take up her time and lead to nothing. Nothing that Josephine concerns herself with seems to lead to anything; and when anything seems to have in it reasonable possibilities of arrival she always shies and scampers by it. I have a feeling that she ought either to take a definite line of her own that promises to bring her out somewhere, or else that she should pay more attention to the possibilities of pairing off. She does neither, but goes on as before, looks handsome, is usually late to breakfast, gets herself good clothes for comparatively little money, pays visits, is kind to the children, makes a great deal of sprightly discourse, and so disposes her energies that every one in the house grumbles when she goes away, and feels a great deal better when she comes home again. She weighs on my conscience. There she is, growing a day older every twenty-four hours and not bettering herself; and she such a likely girl, and in such active demand!

When she got out of school, I was for having her perfect herself in some definite employment

Josephine

—stenography and type-writing, or bookbinding, or even teaching—and at that time she could actually have got a job to teach the younger girls in the school she was leaving. But Cassandra (that is her mother's name; she's my cousin-in-law) said, "Oh no; don't pin her down to any occupation yet; let her see the world." So out she went into the pasture; plenty of grass and nothing to do, except to trot around the ring now and then on exhibition days, which she did with good-will and a fine show of spirits.

I have consulted Saunders, the school-master, about her teaching school. "Must she?" he asked. I admitted that there was no urgent bread-and-butter need of it as yet, but wouldn't it be praiseworthy and wholesome? He demurred. His is a girls' school, and he knows something about fitting girls to make a living. Too many girls *had* to, he said. And then, do you know, he disparaged all my purposes about Josephine, pooh-poohed my misgivings, and talked about the need of saving some of the fine girls who were extra-illustrated and otherwise interesting, to pursue the vitally important business of making life pleasant. "I'll take her gladly," said Saunders. "She'd be ever so pleasant in the school; but don't let her come. There are other Macedonias that need her help more."

She isn't mine, anyhow. She has a full set of parents. My cousin Alexis is living—yes, very much. But he is much more engrossed in making a living than I am, and I know more about girls and their obligations to society than he does. He doesn't seem to care a hang about their obligations to society, nor overmuch about their futures. He has boys in his family, and I suppose planning remunerative futures for his boys takes all the strategical ability he can spare from his immediate business. Never mind. I am going to do something for Josephine myself.

She fools away too much time on ineligibles and men whom there is no chance of her wanting—elderly married men, especially. The fatuity of it! The perversity! I dare say it is restful to a girl whose cousin is trying to marry her off to know a few responsible, agreeable,

unmarriageable old creatures who won't be setting traps for her. But I remonstrate with her
about wasting her sweetness on such persons.
Of course they are attractive, with their records
and perfectly formed manners and all that, but
—"My gracious, Josephine," says I, "don't set
your heart on getting a ready-made man, bitted
and bridle-wise and all that! For shame!
Think of the labor it has cost those old creatures'
wives to bring them to such a stage of amenity
and discipline! Go catch a colt and train him
for yourself, and have something that you can
really call your own."

Well, I'm making a dinner-party for her, and
asking Henry Hawkins and Gresham Clinton.
At least she shall inspect the ranks.

It was a nice dinner. Gertrude took an interest, and when she really takes an interest her
dinners do very well. Gertrude—she's not the
cook, by-the-way; she's my wife; and it was
rather amiable of her to take hold so heartily;
for though she likes Josephine, she does not
share my solicitude about her future. We had

two other girls to dine, Mary Watkins and Alice Blake. I suppose that was a mistake. One other girl would have been better—not too handsome and not too bright. But I should have had to talk to her; and self-sacrifice, even in a cousin, may be overdone. Molly Watkins is no trouble to talk to; and, anyhow, Josephine can hold her own in any company, and better in good company than dull. There is something in shining by contrast, but you get a higher candle-power by competition. Dick Lee was the other man. I didn't ask him on grounds of eligibility, but merely because he fitted in. He doesn't seem to get down to serious and remunerative business very fast, though he is an able fellow, and, I suppose, an able architect, as well as agreeable in discourse. Clinton, it seems, arranged with Jo to drive with him on his brake in the park on Thursday, and threatens to teach her to drive a four-in-hand. She is going to the country with Hawkins and his sister in his new devil-wagon Friday or Saturday, and I think there was a plan for Lee to show her the new cathedral—which

Josephine

seemed unnecessary, as any one can go up there and see what there is of it without any showing.

Gertrude wanted to know why I asked Hawkins, and professed not to see so very much in him. He sat next to her. I explained to her about his qualifications, real and personal, including easements and hereditaments. She admitted that there was more in him than she supposed. She wanted to know where Clinton got his hands. She has known Clinton for ten years, and never made any comment about his hands before. I wonder what ails them, if anything? I told her they came down to him with the rest of his effects. If he got them from his grandfather, they are likely to be useful to him in helping himself to what he wants and holding on to it.

Cassandra has been questioning me about Clinton. I had to tell all I knew—pedigree, record, habits, disposition—and I don't know why, except that Clinton had stopped in to afternoon tea the day before, and got asked to come back the next night to dinner. I believe

137

some of them went with him to the theatre. She wanted to know almost as much about Harry Hawkins. It seems he has a saddle-mare that he wants Josephine to try. Had I known him long? His mother was a Simmons. What Simmons? Was it true that he was born in Chicago? Was it true that he had race-horses? What church did he go to? What church would he be apt to go to if he went? Did I like him? Had his father and mother lived happily together? What was his step-mother like? My replies were based on information and belief, pieced out with surmise. I hope they were satisfactory, though I was stumped to give his step-mother a character, as she has lived in Paris since his father's death.

To-day I met Aunt Emily Doddridge at Tickgood's bookstore, and she asked me to ride up to the park with her in her victoria. She also wished to inquire. She had heard there were two young men who seemed interested in Josephine, and that they were friends of mine. Were they good young men, and did I think their attentions were serious? I replied that, so far as I knew, no young men were good— certainly none so good that there was not room for Josephine to improve them if she cared to undertake the work. As for Clinton and Hawkins, they were solvent, anyhow, and if Josephine cared to experiment with either of them, there would be enough available capital to insure that the experiment would be conducted under reasonably favorable conditions. That was all. Beyond that they seemed sound as yet in wind and limb, and passed for reputable citizens, and there were no judgments out against them, and their credit, socially and fiscally, seemed excellent. I knew no more about them than everybody knew who knew them as well as I did, and that was no more than intelligent observation would yield to any one.

Aunt Emily excused herself for inquiring so explicitly, but explained that she depended a great deal on Josephine, who was the light of her eyes—which now required glasses—and though she would not put so much as a splinter

in the way of her marrying if she saw fit, she
really would not know how to get on without
her. Her house at Bar Harbor, Aunt Emily
maintained, would be a mere receiving-vault
without Jo, and she doubted if she would have
the courage to open it next summer if she must
live in it alone. And as for the winter—well,
there was no use of going too far into particulars,
but she confessed in confidence that she had
hoped that if Josephine did marry, she would
marry some thoroughly desirable poor young
man, who would need help in supporting her,
especially in the summer. Now, did I think
she was likely to take up with a rich man, who
would want to own her, soul, body, and boots,
and monopolize all her time? because, if I did,
it was time for Jo's aunt Emily to have some
shrubs set out in her lot in the cemetery at
Guildfield, and try to make her long home more
attractive.

Now Aunt Emily is a dear lady, and fond of
sport, and I am fond of her. She worked upon
my feelings so that by the time we reached the
park I could hardly command my voice. I fell

Josephine

to with both hands and reassured her, protest-
ing that there was no immediate fear of her
losing Jo; that Hawkins and Clinton were merely two fat pleasure-seekers who liked charming
and amusing girls, much as Aunt Emily herself
did, but were much too timid and old and sel-
fish and prudent to want to marry anybody.
They wouldn't marry, I told her, until they had
tried everything else and got tired of it, and
that wouldn't happen for another ten years,
since they had just begun with autos, and had
not yet tried air-ships. Josephine was much
too good for either of them, and was doubtless
aware of it, but, having time on her hands, and
an accommodating nature, was not averse to
playing with them so long as they continued to
be diverting. Selecting a husband, I said,
usually involved a process of elimination, and
it seemed to be important that an attractive
girl like Jo should not lack fit and various ma-
terial to eliminate. Of course a woman who
selects a husband out of a theoretically possible
fifty thinks he is the pick of the lot, and values
him the more for being so (though he never is);

The Courtship of a Careful Man

and so it had seemed to me to be a sort of service to Josephine to supply her duly and betimes with convenient means of comparison, to enable her, if ever her heart should go out to a truly desirable man, to appreciate how good he was and take him.

I think that by the time Aunt Emily dropped me out on the corner by the club on her way home, she felt considerably happier, but I was a good deal prostrated; and meeting Clinton in the club, I had one with him; and when Hawkins came in and also asked me, I had another with him, which was one more than my habit calls for, and the one they had with me made three. They are still kindly disposed towards me, anyhow, which they might not be if they had heard my conversation with Aunt Emily.

While I was getting lunch to-day down in the subcellar of the Adjustable Building—and of all the bad lunch-places, that is the most odd, and of all eating habits, the habit of eating there is the most inexplicable—Alexis came in and sat down in the vacant seat at my little table.

Josephine

He looked over the programme of food, groaned, and ordered lamb-stew, on the principle of wanting to know the worst.

"Robert," said he, "who's that young Lee who comes to our house, and makes himself so agreeable?"

"I dun'no'," said I. "He isn't mine."

"Well, Jo met him at your house, didn't she?"

"He dined there one night when she did. I ought to have fenced him off, I suppose, but I couldn't. But I deny all responsibility. He's just a man whom Josephine met."

"Why, what's the matter with him? He's a good fellow, isn't he?"

"Lovely, I guess. I don't know."

"How long have you known him?"

"About fifteen years."

"Where's his family?"

"In Baltimore."

"Reputable people, aren't they?"

"Those that are Lees are Lees, and usually Carrolls and Custises on the mother's side. At least I think so. Try the *Social Regulator*. Why?"

The Courtship of a Careful Man

"That wasn't the line of information I was after. I just wondered if he was straight and could make a living."

"I think he makes his own, though I'm not sure. He's an architect. I never knew much about architects, but some of them make livings; so do some painters. I don't know how, but they do. I've seen them have money. I'll inquire about Lee's business, if you want me to."

"Oh no; my interest in him is not so exacting as that. I just wondered; that's all; because Jo seems to find him agreeable. So do I. He *is* agreeable, darn him! and a good fellow, I judge. But why borrow trouble? Stocks seem stronger again to - day. Amalgamated's got quite a head of steam on. Well, I'm glad I'm not fooling with the Street just now."

Lee too; that's almost too much. They sha'n't lay *him* to me, anyhow. He was pure accident. Just to satisfy my own curiosity I'll ask Corbin if Lee can make a living, but I sha'n't tell Alexis. Let him find out for himself. But Josephine? Oh, I've done my best and considerably more for Josephine. I leave her in

144

the Lord's hands, and if she should marry poor it will suit Aunt Emily, anyway.

When I came into the long room of the club this afternoon, Clinton went out the other door. I spoke to Robinson and Brown, and then went to look for him, but he had left the club. My impression was that he avoided me. I hope not. Hawkins was there. He was in good spirits, and we played cowboy pool, and before I went home I made a bridge engagement with him. He said he'd get Clinton and some one else.

Played bridge with Hawkins. He said Clinton couldn't come. Clinton seemed out of sorts, he thought, and talked of going abroad on Saturday. Hatfield and Gibbons were there. Bridge is a good deal calumniated as a game of mischance, but it does eat up time. I had to play, though. I cling to Hawkins, and could not refuse him.

I understand Hawkins has gone to Japan. I did not see him before he went. Hatfield saw him. Hatfield says he meant to stop in Manila and look about, and come home by way of Suez at his leisure, stopping possibly in Constantinople and those parts, if the rumpus now threatening thereabouts matured. He expressed satisfaction in being foot-loose, and said he might change his plans and try the Siberian Railroad. Hatfield said he sniffed battle in the Balkans afar off, like a prudent old war-horse who purposed to get there by the long way, and view the sport, if there was any, from a safe distance. I suspect that Hawkins became conscious of danger at home, and ran away like a wise man while he could. Clinton's retreat doubtless had its effect on him. Bully for old Hawkins! He won't lay anything up against *me*, anyhow. But he might have said good-bye. Maybe he daren't wait.

Josephine dined with us to-night. I told the maid to put the chain on the door, and not to let any man into the house. She dined just with Gertrude and me and the children. "That's what I like best," said Josephine; "just you and Cousin Gertrude and the children, and nobody

146

"JOSEPHINE DINED WITH JUST GERTRUDE AND ME AND THE CHILDREN TO-NIGHT"

Josephine

else." Well, she was delightful; my little girls held her hands till they went to bed, and she did me good, till my affection for her came back almost in full force. I asked whether it was she who had driven Clinton out of town. Not she. No, indeed. Had Mr. Clinton really gone abroad? What took him there, and so suddenly? She felt quite lost without him; he and Mr. Hawkins had done lots of pleasant things for her, quite on my account, she was sure, and she felt deeply indebted to me for putting her in their way. I asked her to credit it to my account, and assured her that they were both quite crazy about me, and would do anything for any girl I pointed out. Did I know where Mr. Hawkins was? She had heard of his being seen in Chicago. I had heard that he had gone West. I asked her if Gertrude's friend Lee was courting her, and she said no; that she understood he was deeply smitten with Eleanor Gay; but she said she saw him now and then, and found him agreeable and informing, and she thanked Gertrude for the advantage of his acquaintance.

147

The Courtship of a Careful Man

Let her have Lee if she likes. I asked Corbin about him, but I sha'n't meddle. But I don't think she'll take him yet a while. I believe she's just a pleasure-seeker like Hawkins and Clinton, and likes the life, and doesn't mean to change it until it begins to wear thin.

Needs a job? No! She's got a job, and works hard at it. She's got Aunt Emily, too, and I wash my hands of responsibility for her future.

Late this afternoon, as I was passing Madison Avenue on a Twenty-ninth Street horse-car, I looked up from my newspaper and casually descried my cousin Josephine half a block away, walking up-town with that man Lee. No doubt I should have gone right on about my business, which was taking me a block farther on, but, acting on the impulse of the moment, I got off the car and condescended to observe them. After all, Josephine is my cousin, and unquestionably dear to me, and I don't know why I should not notice her in the street, no matter whom she is walking with. She seemed in very

cheerful spirits; so did Lee. I observed that
they noticed all the apartment - houses they
passed, and seemed to discuss them, and looked
down the side streets both ways, pausing sometime to do so more thoroughly. They may
have been discussing the progress of domestic
architecture; of course I don't know, but their
talk certainly seemed to concern human habita-
tions, and it certainly looked to me like rather
intimate kind of talk. Not being in a hurry, I
let my Fifth Avenue errand go, and sauntered
up Madison. At Thirty-fourth Street they bore
off towards Park Avenue, and then self-respect
constrained me to turn towards Fifth and go
to the club. Nothing that I noticed — that
forced itself, I should say, on my notice—had
any real significance, and yet somehow I fear
the worst. They seemed so deplorably cheerful, and turned to each other so needlessly
often, that it reminded me, a block away, of
walks that I had taken with Gertrude—I think
it—yes, it certainly was Gertrude—during the
preliminary period of our attachment. I wished heartily that I had had Gertrude along to

149

The Courtship of a Careful Man

give me the benefit of her surmises, but, after all, my impulse to get off the car would not have been strong enough to have moved her, too; and besides that, I had the feeling that the apparition of those young people was confidential—a circumstance proper enough for my personal observation, but hardly suitable to be pointed out.

Corbin came into the club while I was there, and I cornered him with the help of a waiter, and artfully led him on, by way of labor unions, strikes, the building industry, and the new Public Library, to architecture and architects, and so worked him carefully down to Lee, of whom he spoke with respect as a man of talent and prospects, and told me of some good work he had done. Gracious! Is it possible that I shall presently be snooping around in such fashion as this to find out what sort of landing there is for my own girls beyond the matrimonial hedge? How dreadfully sordid such anxieties make one!

I hear that Lee's plans have won in the United Art Societies' competition for their new exhibition building. That is a first-class suc-

cess, Corbin says, though he tells me the money
for the building is not all subscribed yet. The
idea was that some good plans would help in
getting subscriptions. I had rather he had a
bona fide commission to build an office-building,
or a hotel—that is, it would seem like better
business, though Heaven knows whether there is
any basis for my absurd concern about Lee's
business. Still, Corbin says this success will go
far to establish his professional standing, and
that he will be sure to get jobs out of it, and
probably some good partnership offers. As an
advertisement, Corbin says, it could hardly be
bettered, and he considers Leé abundantly able
to deliver all the goods it calls for.

Well, the fat is in the fire now. Last night
I got this letter:

"DEAR COUSIN ROBERT,—You will hear with relief,
but perhaps not entirely with surprise—you are such a
particularly observing cousin—that I am engaged to
Richard Lee. I stipulated that it should be left to
me to break it to you, and if the blue stamp carries this
letter as promptly as it should, you and Cousin Gertrude will be the first persons outside of this house to

be informed. We consider you our ally in this en-
tanglement, and I rely very much upon your help in
getting Aunt Emily Doddridge's consent. Father and
mother are resigned, and, I hope, satisfied. As for
you and Cousin Gertrude, we count with confidence
on your felicitations.   Your affectionate,

"JOSEPHINE."

Of course there is nothing for it now but to
make the best of it. It was none of my doing,
but I don't know that it is any the worse job
because of that. Josephine seemed cheerful,
even pleased, over it. When I saw that she
was fully committed I burned my bridges and
went in to make things as easy as I could for
her. Cassandra was resigned; Alexis philo-
sophical. He said Lee had had an excellent
partnership offered to him, and would probably
take it. None of them showed elation, but
neither did any of them disparage Josephine's
choice. They would have felt the same, I
think, whomever Josephine had taken, except
that if they hadn't liked the man they would
have felt worse. I will say for Lee, darn him!
that he is a comfortable being to have about,
and an acquisition to any family. It wasn't

152

Josephine

that they liked him less, but that they liked Jo more. But, after all, it isn't as though she were going to live in China.

They asked me to go over to see Aunt Emily, which I did. She was tearful and dejected. She understood, she said, that this Mr. Lee was a friend of mine. I said that any friend of Josephine's was a friend of mine, but that my acquaintance with Mr. Lee was not yet intimate, and that Gertrude knew him better than I. But she went on and searched me for information about him, moaning all the time at the thought of losing Josephine. "Oh, well, aunt," said I, "try to look upon it more as an investment. I have faith to believe that there will still be something coming to us from Josephine even if she does marry. If we could keep her along always just about twenty-five and no older, and with life and its possibilities always ahead of her, that would be one thing. But you know what precarious property girls are, and how indifferently some girls keep, and with what inexorable certainty possibilities that are not realized slip by." I went on to speak of

153

the advantages of the common lot, and of family life, and having a man of your own in the house. "But what shall I do with my house at Bar Harbor?" said Aunt Emily. "Sell it," said I, "and hire Lee to build you another nearer town. He can do it. You know he is in that business. And perhaps, if you encourage him, he'll build one near by for Josephine."

Whether that is a practical suggestion I know not, but it sent Aunt Emily's mind off on another tack, and that was something. For impecunious young persons about to marry, a doting and affluent aunt may be an exceedingly helpful property. All young couples who attempt to set up housekeeping in New York need one or two established homes to fall back upon in times of stress, and especially a country home not too far from town, where babies can be sent in the spring.

Clinton's back. We played cowboy pool from half-past five to quarter of seven to-day, and it was like old times. What a fool a man is who can't mind his own business!

Found: a Situation

Found: a Situation

LISS CLARKSON had been a successful lawyer in New York. He had worked hard for thirty - five years, had earned great fees by honorable service, and, strange to say, had shown more than ordinary gumption in the investment of his surplus funds. Good lawyers are not very apt to be good men of business for themselves, but it so happened that Mr. Clarkson had a sort of business instinct that served him as well in his own concerns as in his labors for his clients. He was not unduly interested in money-making, but when it came to a question of where he should put the money he had, he showed a very pretty talent for putting it where it would breed.

The Courtship of a Careful Man

Then he let it alone, and usually it did breed. His chief entertainment he found in the practice of law, and being suited by a scale of living that he had adopted when his income was still modest, he stuck pretty close to it all his life. Evidently he was a fortunately constituted person, as men go, and yet he made one very serious mistake, for being well adapted to live happily and usefully, as well as profitably, on this earth, for as many score years as human perishability ordinarily permits, he let his work crowd him a little too hard.

To keep alive and in the best working order in New York is a very fine art, which is practised to admiration by many expert workers. It is a matter of so many months in town, so many out of town but near by, so many weeks of clear rest in Europe or somewhere, so much horse exercise, so much golf, so many Saturdays away from the office. Age is a bad disease, and finally a fatal one, and the sort of hard head-work that strains the nerves is another, and the man who works his wits hard in a great city has to fortify himself watchfully against both. **Mr.**

Found : a Situation

Clarkson was duly kind and indulgent to himself, especially when his wife insisted, and he golfed on occasion, and had been seen on a horse, and he had rested himself, first or last, in convenient places all the way from the head waters of the Nile to the Sandwich Islands. He intended to be prudent, and he usually did what the duty of self-preservation seemed to demand. But sometimes crises in the affairs of his clients kept him up to his eyes in labors and responsibilities long after his rest-time had come. It is not healthy to go on after you are tired, and the older you grow the more unhealthy it is. Mr. Clarkson did it once too often, and died at fifty-four, leaving a disconsolate widow, a boy in college, two grown girls, and about a million and a half of dollars. Half of this fortune went outright to his wife; the other half he directed should presently go to his children.

The boy was a good boy, well born and well beloved, well schooled, and trained as soundly as intelligence and affection could compass. When the clasp of the good hand that had held his relaxed, he kept on in the path that had been marked out for him. He went on through college, graduated creditably, and took ship for Europe to join his mother and sisters, who had started earlier in the season. Julien Hatfield, a classmate, shared his state-room. Judge and Mrs. Finch were aboard. He knew them, as he knew several others of his shipmates, as family friends, and he and Hatfield found acquaintances of their own besides. To be twenty-one years old, and just out of a great college, and to have your face turned towards Europe with nothing more perplexing in hand for immediate consideration than how best to look at and enjoy the great world, is not at all a bad situation. James Clarkson liked it. The only thing that bothered him at all was the choice of an occupation.

"Charles," said Mrs. Finch, from her deck-chair to her husband, "what is that young Clarkson going to do?"

"I don't know. Be a joy and comfort to his mother, I hope. He's just out of college."

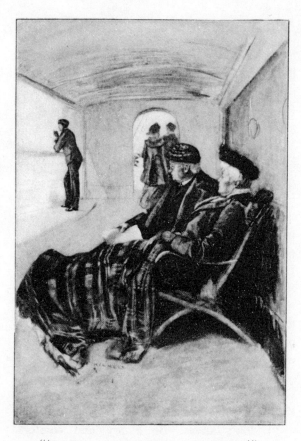

"'I THINK YOU HAD BETTER TALK TO HIM'"

Found: a Situation

"Yes, I know. Well, what is he going to do next?"

"He hasn't told me. Why, his father left him enough to live on, and he has more coming to him eventually from his mother. Do you think he ought to find a job?"

"What do *you* think?"

"Every good American has to have a job. That's one of our national defects. But there seems to be no urgent haste in James Clarkson's case. I'd like to be a young creature just out of college and on my way to Europe with money in my pocket; wouldn't you?"

"I dare say, and yet it seems to me rather a critical situation. The boy has no father."

"He's got a mighty good mother."

"I dare say she'll spoil him. We all love to spoil our boys. That's too good a boy to waste. I think you had better talk to him."

And the judge, being a dutiful husband, sat down next to James Clarkson in the smoking-room that evening.

"James," said he, "are you staying long abroad?"

The Courtship of a Careful Man

"Two or three months, judge, anyway. I suppose it will depend upon mother's plans. She engaged her passage home in September, but she may change her mind. The girls will probably want her to stay all winter."

"I suppose Europe is a fairly good place for girls for a while, but delays are dangerous, and I have known delays in Europe to have pretty serious consequences to girls as attractive as your sisters. How do you feel about it, as the man of the family?"

"I haven't had a large experience in keeping girls out of mischief. I'd like to look about a bit over there myself."

"Have you any plans for the fall? Are you going to study a profession?"

"Father expected me to study law, but going into the law with father was one thing, and going into it on my own account is another."

"The law is still a respectable profession. Livings are still made at it; but I don't know that the problem of making a living presses very hard as yet on you."

"I have not suffered yet for lack of neces-

saries. I'd just as lief study law, but when it
comes to going down-town and practising it—
What do you think, judge? Would it pay?"

"Men make it pay, James, who have to. But
it isn't the only calling. There's medicine. I
invited my son to study law, but he liked doctoring better. Have you any taste that way?"

"I have not discovered yet that I have a
strong bent towards anything."

"Did you do any work in college?"

"I didn't hurt myself, but I worked decently.
It pleased father to have me do it respectably,
and I got the habit of it."

"What do you think you learned?"

"A little about things in general. I scattered
a good deal. Father's idea was to have me get
a general education and specialize later."

"Let's employ the method of elimination in
your problem. You haven't got to do anything in a hurry. You won't be a doctor. I
judge that you won't be any kind of engineer
or man of science, nor go into the army or navy,
nor go on the stage. That leaves you law,
politics, diplomacy, finance, art, literature,

newspapers, business, and the life of leisure. How about the life of leisure? Would that suit you?"

"I guess so, for a while; but don't you think it's pretty dull in the long run?"

"They say it's very much helped out by sport."

"Do you think there is much in that, judge?"

"*I* think that if a man is going to make a business of anything, it had better be work, for if he makes a business of play, what is he going to turn to for recreation? Besides, leisure and sport are pretty dear. Could you afford it?"

"I have got plenty enough to live on now."

"But you might marry and have children. It often happens so. I dare say you have enough to support a family, but I doubt if you have enough to support a family and an idle man, too. To maintain an idle man to his satisfaction costs a good deal. And some of your money may get away from you. I have known that to happen, too. Be on the safe side, and try to qualify yourself to make a

Found: a Situation

living. At any rate, work hard at something, and get interested enough in it to find a satisfactory occupation in your work. A workingman can feel rich on an income on which a man of leisure feels poor."

"That sounds like good advice, judge, but I don't yet see my way clear enough to know what I want to do."

"That isn't strange, for most men are pushed into their life's work by circumstances and necessity, and you haven't the pinch of need to help you."

"Father's plan was that I should study law."

"Well, study law, whether you practise it or not. It won't hurt you to learn some law, even though eventually you come to be a minister, or a banker, or a railroad man, or enlist and go to a war. Law's a good subject; only, whatever you take hold of, take hold hard."

"I'm going to look about a bit first."

"You can't do better, but don't do it too long."

The judge finished his cigar and went out.

165

The Courtship of a Careful Man

Julien Hatfield came up and took the seat he had left.

"You look thoughtful, Jimmy. Don't think; it's bad for you, particularly in vacation-time. Has the judge been scolding you?"

"The judge talks of putting me to work."

"All in good time. What at?"

"To study law, for a starter."

"Law's a pretty long row. You could go back to the Law School, though; that would be fair sport, though they work like nailers there."

"I don't think I could. Mother would want me to stay in New York. I'd have to go to the Columbia School."

"I suppose they'd let you work hard there if you insisted. And after three years of it, when you've learned the rudiments, where are you?"

"Still in New York."

"Yes, and you go into an office down-town and get a job as clerk, and in the course of ten years or so you get to be managing clerk maybe, and years after that you get so you can make a living. And whenever you want to go any-

Found: a Situation

where you can't leave the office, and if you
don't work yourself to death, you don't get
anywhere, and if you work yourself to death, you
don't have any fun. Better go into a bank or
be a broker."

"A bank, yes, and stunt your mind figuring
interest. As for being a broker, there's more in
roulette, and it's just as respectable."

"No, it isn't. There's no money in roulette
unless you run the dive, and that isn't respectable. You may get pulled, for roulette is il-
legal. But brokers who run a fair game can't
be pulled. Every few days maybe they buy
or sell something for a real investor, and that
leavens all the gamb'es."

"I'm not going to be a broker, anyhow."

"I dare say you'll do worse. It's the easiest
trade to learn there is, and you have money
enough to buy a seat."

"That's reason enough for not doing it.
Don't you know the story of the Arkansas man
and the saw-mill?"

"Tell it."

"He wrote to inquire the price of a saw-mill
167

The Courtship of a Careful Man

that would do certain specified stunts, and cut
so many boards a day. The manufacturers
wrote him that it would cost sixteen hundred
dollars. He wrote back, 'If a man had sixteen
hundred dollars, what in thunder would he
want of a saw-mill?'"

"Pshaw! Jimmy, you are not of an aspiring
nature."

"Yes, I am, but stock-broking wouldn't help
me realize my aspirations. I don't aspire to
be a banker, nor to own railroads, and for the
moment I am not hard put to it to make a
living."

"What *is* your lay, anyhow?"

"Just to take notice for a while, and find out
what's going on, and try to get ready to take
hold somewhere. By-the-way, Julien, we must
get to know those girls at the captain's table."

"The Markham girls? Very pleasing ladies.
That's their aunt they're with. But they're
getting along all right. They don't need us."

"Maybe not, but I am out to take notice, and
I notice those girls."

168

Found: a Situation

"Sail in; your friends the Finches know them. They'll put you on."

Now the elder Miss Markham was a grown-up person, no less than twenty-two years old, and with vested interests in life and society which occupied a good part of her energies, and left her with only a limited share of attention to bestow on a youth just out of college. But Edith Markham was four years younger, and in college herself.

"We had to wait for her," Miss Julia Markham explained to James. "Burnmore takes no note of the wishes of relatives, and doesn't let out until it gets ready."

"Never mind. You'll have a good month of London left if you want it. My mother and sisters are to meet me there."

"We don't want a month, but I think we'll take a fortnight. We're going to Scotland."

"Now I hope my mother means to take me to Scotland. She is keeping my plans hid until I join her, under pretence of consulting me."

"I remember your sisters at Miss Perkin's school. You must remember them, Edith

They were nearer your age; a little older than you and younger than I."

"I beg to offer you my sympathy in having the responsibility of a younger sister. I have two, as you know, and only mother to help me raise them."

"I have plenty of help with Edith—father and mother, and at present Aunt Sarah; but still it is a charge."

"You are sending her to college, which is more than I am doing for my sisters. What drove you to that? Was her intelligence so defective as to need further cultivation, or so rare that nothing less than all the knowledge going could satisfy it?"

"You'll have to ask her. It wasn't I that sent her to college. She would go, and, being her father's pet, she did go."

"Defective intelligence," said Edith. "Scarce, not rare. That was the trouble, Mr. Clarkson. It was a case of a desperate appeal to art to help out nature."

"You are a sophomore now, aren't you? I never met a girl sophomore before. I beg your

"WE ARE NOT FRIVOLOUS, LIKE YOU MEN"

pardon, but you don't seem to me nearly so rudimentary as the men sophomores are. Do you know very much yet? Have you a class yell, and can you smoke cigarettes?"

"I know too much to tell. Don't trifle with me like that. I am a serious person. We all take education seriously at Burnmore. We are not frivolous like you men."

"Are you on the basket-ball team?"

"Not yet. Were you on the nine?"

"I am surprised that you should have to ask. Don't they let you read the papers at Burnmore? Try to remember seeing my picture in the Sunday *Screech*."

"We don't take the Sunday *Screech* at Burnmore, and I don't remember your picture. We only take grave papers, and no Sunday papers at all. Our papers only print pictures of politicians and labor leaders and people of consequence."

"Then I'm afraid you haven't seen mine. And, indeed, I dare say the Sunday papers will print your picture many times before they print mine again, for I have passed out of public life into eclipse, and you—even if you escape the basket-ball team and that grade of illustration —are pretty sure to ornament the 'society pages' a little later. You see, a man jumps from college into outer darkness, but a girl emerges into the strong light that beats upon a bud."

"Do you hear that bugle? That's dinnêr."

"Do college girls take thought of anything so intellectual as food?"

"They have to. Soup, meat, and vegetables are required courses."

"And pie and candy electives, I suppose. I congratulate you both on your interest in all of them on shipboard."

Acquaintance ripens fast aboard an Atlantic liner. James found no better occupation than to chatter, when occasion offered, with Edith Markham, and occasion offered several times a day for the three days of the voyage that were left. Edith was nothing loath to chat with James.

"Don't you like him?" she asked her sister.

Found: a Situation

"He seems a pleasant youth, and has more ideas than one would naturally expect in a man just out of college. Has he told you what he proposes to make of himself?"

He had not, Edith said. As to that, she had neither inquired nor wondered; but the question being suggested to her, she turned it over in her mind. It is one of the two questions which consideration of a new graduate inevitably invites. What is he? is the first one, and when some conclusion has been reached about that the other is bound to follow.

James gave himself no concern about Edith's future beyond its immediate developments, but with those he did concern himself. He discussed London hotels with Miss Sarah Markham, and recommended the one where his mother was staying. The plans of people bent on pleasure are easily adjusted to include anything that promises to be pleasant. The Markham ladies and the Clarkson ladies found each other profitable company in London, made some explorations in common, dined together sometimes, shared knowledge and swapped suggestions, and found themselves suited to a good deal of harmonious co-operation. A family party is usually improved by the infusion of suitable intruders, and two family parties that happen to be congenial may be mingled, to the advantage of both. The summer aims of the Clarksons and the Markhams were substantially alike; common acquaintances turned up daily, and, without merging, they drifted in relations of confidence.

So it came about without cost of much contrivance on James's part that he found himself on an August evening sitting in the twilight with Edith Markham in the window of a Princess Street hotel in Edinburgh. They were talking with the ease of familiar friends.

"How is Burnmore going to seem to you," he asked her, "after this pleasant, idle summer? Do you think you will ever get down to work again?"

"Oh yes, and I shall like it. The summer is doing me good. Father and mother start from London, you know, to-night, and when they get here I shall like it better still. But I shall be glad to go home with them."

"Burnmore can't be half bad, if you like it so well. What put it into your head to go there?"

"My teachers, partly, and circumstances. I planned years ago to go there. Didn't you always mean to go to college?"

"Yes; but college isn't so much a matter of course for girls yet."

"Do you think I could have done better?"

"Oh no, but you know plenty already, and you have three more years of studies ahead of you. Think how superior you'll be when you are completely educated. What are you going to do then?"

"I haven't got to that yet. You have been through college and are completely educated; what are you going to do?"

"I knew you'd come to that sometime. Everybody does. I have even come to it myself. I know I've got to find a job. It's different with a girl—with you at least. Even when you get out of college nobody will insist that *you* shall find a job. You'll just go on and pour tea, and slum, and make calls, and shop, and dance, and go to dinners, and adorn house-parties like the other girls."

"Isn't it a dreadful prospect? What would you do about it?"

"Don't ask me. I don't think it will be so bad. I think I would be a loafer if it were not for my congenital compunctions. You see, I am a working-man's son, and suffer from the natural moral inconveniences of that derivation."

"Gracious! you wouldn't want to be idle, would you? Why, you'd never come to anything! You wouldn't even hold your own. You'd degenerate."

"Yes; that's the awkward part of it. Not but what degeneration might be a pleasant enough process for a good many years to come!"

"Oh no! It would be—oh, it would be just disgusting. It would be losing one's own soul, and not even getting the whole world."

"Awful! But I wouldn't have to go head-long to the demnition bowwows. I could buy a farm, and raise pigs and horses, and travel a

little, and go hunting, and fish, and keep in
physical health, anyway. Would you have me
go into business and lose my inheritance trying
to do something without learning how?"

"Why not learn how to do something?"

"I must, of course, but what? How are you
going to stand off degeneration when you get
through with Burnmore?"

"I don't know, but somehow. I'm not going
to dawdle."

"Well, I tell you. I'm going to look around,
and if I find anything that needs doing that's
about your size, I'll let you know. And if you
notice any likely job that's about my size,
please remember me. It would be a high privilege to be of use to a lady in such straits as you
are facing; and as for myself, you see, my
troubles are already on me, and it would be a
work of mercy to throw me a line."

"And meanwhile are you going to drift about
and wait to be rescued?"

"Alas! I am not. I am going to take my
mother and the girls to Paris, where they propose, as you know, to spend the fall acquiring

French and fineries, and in just about a month
I shall take ship for New York with Julien Hatfield and immerse myself into the study of the
law. Much good may I do law and law do me!
It is the thing nearest to hand. I suppose you'll
be in town for the holidays?"

"Oh yes."

"And again in the spring, and I trust I may
be able from time to time to command the advantage of your venerable and learned counsel."

"It is not polite of you to make fun of
me!"

"And I shall be on the lookout for a job for
you. Do they teach short-hand at Burnmore?
That sometimes leads to excellent employ-
ments."

"It does, really. There are girl stenographers
in father's office, and, if worse should come to
worst, I could learn short-hand and hire out to
him. But I didn't know your plans were all
made!"

"No? They weren't. They were under consideration until to-night, and we have just settled them."

Found: a Situation

Three years pass quickly when there is nothing to hinder. Once James Clarkson had buc-
kled to the study of law, they sped fast enough
for him. He took hold hard, as is proper for a
law student, and fairly bent himself to lay the
foundations of professional knowledge. And besides learning law, he began the serious study
of his own town and the people in it. It was
only serious in the sense that he paid real attention to it, keeping his eyes and his mind open,
cultivating old acquaintances and picking up
many new ones; observing, reflecting, getting
his bearings little by little in the great world,
and enjoying life very much in the process.
There is no royal road to law any more than to
any other branch of learning. Shirk the work,
and you miss the results; but along any road
one may live by the way, and James was able
to do that to excellent advantage. Coming
from a great university, he had a ready-made
set of familiar friends. His new studies made
him other associations and acquaintances, and
the social distractions which abound for likely
young persons in a great city were always ready

The Courtship of a Careful Man

to nibble at his time and abbreviate his hours of
sleep. But one of the advantages of having a
steady and imperious job is that it serves as a
protection against importunate distractions,
social or otherwise; and any one who kept faithful tab on James might have noticed that when
he was seen at a dance, it always happened to
be vacation-time in the colleges, and particularly
at Burnmore.

It had come to be the Easter vacation in
Edith Markham's last year in college. Central
Park is not exuberantly springlike in March,
but even then it begins to show vernal anticipa-
tions; and, as at all other times, it is a place to
which young people not too experienced, who are
disposed to walk out together, may profitably
turn. Our young people were turning it to account, and were skirting the edge of the reservoir.

"You know," said James, "that I promised
to look out for a job for you when you got out
of college."

"And I for you, but *I* have had no chance to
look."

Found: a Situation

"No, not yet; but now that you are coming back into the world, I shall expect substantial help from you."

"What have you done for me? You have been here all this time, and looked about, I suppose."

"Yes; looked about some, but there was no use of my finding you anything until you were ready to take it."

"That sounds a little like an excuse, but it won't work much longer. In June I become a finished product, and June is only three months off."

"And in June or thereabouts I shall become an attorney and counsellor at law, and shall expect you to discover a suitable opening for my talents and learning."

"You will! But you told me you were going in a law-office down-town."

'I am, but that does not let you out. A law-office is only a point to stand on. What am I to go there for? What am I to try to do, and how, and for whom am I to do it?"

"Isn't there work to be done in law-offices?
181

The Courtship of a Careful Man

Sha'n't you do work and earn money there like other people? Won't you go on learning to apply the knowledge you have got? It's plain sailing for you, as I see it; but think of me, full of acquired wisdom, and nothing definite to do with it unless I teach school."

"Were you thinking of doing that?"

"Really, I wish I might, but they wouldn't let me teach school until I had had a chance to see society and the polite world; and I suppose by the time I have been two years in society, and devoted myself to the entertainment of young gentlemen like you, I shall have forgotten so much, and fallen into such lazy habits, that no school will have me. I think my case is far more desperate than yours. Indeed, I don't think yours is desperate at all. You have only to go right on, and follow your own leanings, and I dare say you will wind up by being chief-justice."

"Pshaw! You don't recognize my predicament. I haven't incentive enough. It will be a long time before I make money enough to pay for the expense and inconvenience of mak-

182

Found: a Situation

ing it. It is very expensive to work in New
York. Food is dear; recreation is dear; rents
are high. It will cost a great deal more than
it will come to at first to be a law-clerk. And
what for? Who's going to be any better off?"

"You! You! You! Why, what a man! You
have got to work, with wages or without. There
is no other way of amounting to anything."

"And I have got to amount to something,
have I? So be it. Now I have an idea. You
see, you are highly competent, and afraid your
energies will run to waste. You need a situation. I am obviously in need of being taken
in hand and driven up the hill Difficulty. I
can't insist that I am the situation that you
need, but I am unquestionably a situation that
needs you. Will you please take it?"

"Take *you*?"

"No less: for better or worse, beginning, if
you would be so good, not very long after Com-
mencement."

"I really think you will do something as a
lawyer, you are so unexpected. But I think
you have an exaggerated impression of the ur-

gency of my needs. Is this all a brand-new idea?"

"Dear lady, don't trifle with a true heart. You know that the idea is pretty nearly three years old, and has worked day and night and Sundays all that time. I may not be much of a situation, but the situation, such as it is, has a lot of your handiwork in it."

"Do you know that that is my hand you are holding?"

"Oh yes. It's ever so comfortable to hold. You wouldn't take it from me, would you? You have known—you must have known— this long time that I loved you. I don't believe you'd be here now if you were not going to let me keep on."

"No? I don't know. Perhaps not. I must have time to think. Anyhow it would be a way to escape 'society.'"

They were married in October.

"Charles," said Mrs. Finch, after the wedding, "what do you think of it?"

"Excellent plan. Charming young people,

184

Found: a Situation

and I would say very likely to hit it off happily. She must be almost James's first love. What kind of a world would it be, do you suppose, if all parents were provident enough to qualify their sons to marry by the first intention (as surgeons say)?"

"Oh, it would be lovely."

"It would certainly be different. Well, there's the making of a very fine woman in Edith. It speaks well for Clarkson that he knew a good thing when he saw it. They can start in now and live a simple, God-fearing, two maids-and-a-furnace-man life in town, and by the time Clarkson needs more income, I dare say he will have learned how to get it. You needn't be afraid he won't work now. I think he has got it in him; but, anyway, the inconvenience of maintaining a family on a fixed income of any reasonable size is so much greater than the inconvenience of working, that I have little fear but that, barring accidents, he will turn out a useful man."

THE END